NORTHERN BEACHES WRITERS' GROUP

The Northern Beaches Writers' Group is an award-winning
writing critique group based in Sydney. We're online at:

northernbeacheswritersgroup.com
facebook.com/northernbeacheswritersgroup

A NOISE ON AN ISLAND

edited by
ZENA SHAPTER

A Noise On An Island

First published in Australia 2018 by
the Northern Beaches Writers' Group, Sydney.

A Cataloguing-in-Publications record for this title is available from
The National Library of Australia.

Cover design by Zena Shapter.

ISBN 978-0-6480765-3-7

The characters in this book are fictitious and any resemblance to real
persons, living or dead, is purely coincidental.

Contents

Noise is unwanted sound, judged to be unpleasant, loud or disruptive to hearing.

At first we cared about the past...

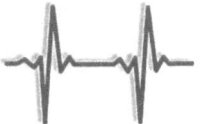

Midnight

Kylie Pfeiffer

Midnight is my favourite time. The stillness of it. The quiet. The island's isolation makes for a dark expansive sky, the Milky Way a bright gash across its depths. At midnight there are no people to give me their flat, suspicious stares, hiding guilt behind accusation.

This midnight is different.

This midnight is filled with the rhythmic shushing of a ventilator and the harsh repetition of a heart monitor. The low grey ceiling of the hospital ward blocks my view of the stars. All I can see through the salt-greasy window is an orange-tinted fragment of sky, its brilliant contrasts muted, diluted by the lights of the mainland. Intensive care unit staff shuffle in and out, their gazes passing through me as they focus on their patients.

My aunt is wired with probes measuring heart rate and blood oxygen. Tubes run in and out, at the crook of her elbow, her nostril, her neck, and from other places hidden by the sheet. The tracheostomy, still red and raw, makes a wet, mechanical wheeze. A trickle of foul-coloured liquid runs to a bag on the side of the bed.

The room is dimly lit, a brighter pool around my aunt from the myriad of screens. Those lights show me my aunt is still alive, still breathing. Each pulse tells me her ugly heart still beats.

Every now and then the nurse comes and pats my shoulder. It takes all of my control not to flinch from her touch. I've never met this nurse before but I want to yell and spit in her face. Why sympathy? Why now? You all knew what my aunt was. You saw my bruises. You pretended I really had fallen down the stairs when I turned up with yet another broken bone. You dealt with me quickly, all bustling efficiency, no eye contact and no questions, then sent me home with her. Were you too lazy or too stupid to do the paperwork? Or was it something else? Was there a thrill in seeing a child broken? And now you pat my shoulder.

It wasn't just the hospital staff. The islanders heard my aunt's wild yelling, understood what the white plaster and bandages concealed. They looked away as they passed, the ground suddenly fascinating. I've thought about what dirty, vile secrets they must've had. Why would they expose my aunt's? Challenge that complicit silence? But I was just a child. How could they not?

I should rage and scream, but tonight I'm filled with a strange joy that leaves me floating. I'm dust motes in sunshine, sailing on an updraft of relief and triumph. The scan of my aunt's head shows the dark patch of blood fanning out from the point where a thin-walled vessel burst its confines. Her brain's putty, even if machines keep her lungs inflating and arteries thrumming. She's as good as dead. Dead before she had the chance to finish me. I could sing.

And I'm her next of kin. I get to decide if she lives or dies. I look at my finger, amazed at the power in that chunk of flesh and bone. The power to keep or destroy. I'm drunk on the thought of ending her now, and yet...

She looks so small and pathetic, filled with tubes. Her jaundiced skin has sunk around her eyes, contracting over sharp-edged cheekbones, pulling at the corners of her mouth, turning her rat-like features skeletally sharp. Her body's so flat she could be part of the bedding. And the smell coming out of her... an acrid mix of decaying flesh and cleaning chemicals. Revulsion crawls across my skin like an army of ants.

My aunt would hate being so vulnerable and exposed, so

completely lacking in power. She'd be desperate, pleading with me to make it stop, please make it stop, please stop. She'd want me to end her humiliation and pain and degradation. She'd want the switch flicked immediately.

But I won't. I've imagined her death so many times but now I can make her suffer like she's made me suffer. I'll leave her plugged in and ticking away, with machines breathing in, breathing out. With nurses and doctors poking and prodding her at all hours, with the indignity of it. Even though her brain's gone, I can tell she registers I'm the one in control now. That I hold the power in just one little finger.

"You alright love?" the nurse asks.

I'm crying.

The nurse puts an arm around my shoulders and her sickly sweet perfume engulfs me. My body goes rigid, but she doesn't seem to notice.

"I know it's hard to see a loved one like this. We've made your aunt comfy and she's not hurting."

I wish they'd stop the pain killers, make her hurt like I've hurt. I strain to smile and blink away my blurry vision. "I'm tired." My voice chokes.

"It's alright love." She looks at the pocket watch dangling on her bosom. "You know, my Bart's running parts out for the cray trawler tonight. He'll be leaving in the next 15 minutes. Why don't you head home and get a good night's sleep in your own bed?" She pats me again. "You can come back over tomorrow."

I nod, moving away from the patting hand. The heart rate monitor continues its insistent, unrelenting noise. Each beep stabs at me, skewering through my eye sockets. Beneath it, driving it, is my aunt's heart, feebly pushing against her ribs.

I'm filled with an urgent need to get away, to be back on the island.

I leave the washed out light and antiseptic smell of the ICU. I shield my eyes from the brightness of the corridor's double line of fluorescents. The automatic doors whoosh open and I escape the frigid air conditioning into the warm night.

Down at the jetty, Bart's readying to launch.

"Can I get a ride out?"

"Nell." He looks me up and down, his eyes raking my skin. "Heard about your aunt."

I will him not to say anything sympathetic. I cross my arms over my chest. "Well?"

"Yeah, no worries. Hop in."

I step aboard and settle into the seat up front, relieved the dual outboards will make conversation impossible.

For the next hour, salt air buffets me, stripping away the heaviness the hospital has deposited over the last few days.

Then I see the dark mass of the island and the tension in my shoulders drops away.

Within minutes I'm stepping off onto the timber jetty, then onto the sand. I'm on solid ground but it feels unsteady, rising and falling like the swell we've just crossed. My ears echo a throbbing rhythm even after the outboards stutter into silence. The smell of the ocean gives way to over-ripe vegetation, rotting in earthy, worm-riddled layers. It's after two in the morning, but the heat is as heavy as a blanket.

I'm wide awake, listening to crickets rustling their wings. Home is not an option. The thought of those damp walls enclosing me has me fighting for breath. Instead I walk, letting the moon guide me along a worn path up into the scrub. Gravel crunches beneath my feet and the exertion and humidity has my dress sticking to my thighs and back.

A void of darkness, deeper and more complete than my surroundings warns me I'm close, then I'm at the edge of the water-filled quarry. The inky black depths suck all the light from the sky, drawing it in, drawing it down until it's lost. The surface appears weighted in oil, thick and viscous. I skirt around to find the steps cut into the side of the bordering cliff and the climb leaves me with a low thumping in my temples. I pause at the top and look down.

The blackness pulls at me, a waiting lover, eager to embrace. It empties me, as it always does. As it has since the day I ran here, a bruise spreading like a stain across my cheek. Snot and tears running down my face.

That was the day Aunt Celia had moved in. Mum had died. I couldn't stop crying, wanting her to come home. Celia had told me to shut up then clubbed my ear. Blood pushed into my head, expanding, thudding against my skull, pounding louder and louder until my aunt heard it too.

"Shut up, shut up, SHUT UP," she'd screamed, her hands slapping in time to the beating inside me. "Stop making that fucking noise!"

And then I was running. Trying to get away from the noise but it was all around me, inside me, chasing me, getting louder until it was on top of me. I couldn't run anymore, couldn't get away, couldn't breathe. Then I saw the quarry, its surface rippling, hypnotic. The water stilled me, calm pouring in with each breath. I could pretend the noise wasn't there.

I can still feel my aunt's hands on me, how they stung my cheeks, my body. Her spit hitting my face. I try to block the old thoughts but the pressure in my head increases, an all too familiar warning. I cover my ears, trying to shield myself, but it doesn't work. The noise builds within me then I hear it trying to get out. It expands to fill the space in and around me, echoing off the cliffs, growing. It's so loud, like a physical blow. Pain grabs at my chest.

How can she do this to me when she's unconscious in a hospital bed?

The noise drums through me, a double-tap, deep and resonant. Celia pulls it from me, extracting it so she can shove it down into the water below. The surface ripples, radiating circles that dissipate against dirt and rock. I stagger back, away from the quarry, away from her, then I'm running until I trip and hit the ground. My teeth punch into my lip and I taste dirt and blood.

In that instant the noise stops. Regular night sounds return. The drone of the mass insect choir, the squabbling of bats in trees, the swoop of wings in still air.

My heart thuds against my ribs. My breath is ragged. But the noise has gone. I pick myself up, hold out a hand in the dim light. It's shaking and I try to hold it still. I give up and brush the dirt from my dress, drawing in big lungfuls of air to steady myself. The familiarity of where I am helps to even me out.

This has always been my safe place. My refuge once I'd learnt which of my aunt's moods were most dangerous. I'd come to visit my grandfather in the old site office, one of those cabins on concrete blocks that was never meant to be permanent. When the quarry was shut down, he lost his job. He took his swag out of his ute, rolled it out on the floor of the office and never returned home. He left his wife and young son to get on with life without him.

Thick vines and scrub have reclaimed the site, almost completely hiding the cabin until I'm in front of it. Pa has covered the rust holes with old sheets of corrugated iron. In daylight, the cabin resembles a brown patchwork quilt in a sea of green, but the moonlight fades it all to grey.

Pa's sitting on the steps, smoking. I've never once found him asleep, no matter what time I've turned up. I sit beside him and let the smoke swirl around me. The smell of his tobacco makes me feel safe. Pa doesn't say anything, doesn't acknowledge the monstrous noise or the unsocial hour of my visit, just sucks on his cigarette, intensifying the glowing ember at its tip. He lets out his breath in a long, white stream and offers me his tobacco pouch with nicotine stained fingers.

I learnt how to roll cigarettes not long after my aunt moved in to look after me. I'd turn up breathless and scared and sit in Pa's cabin to roll one after another, neatly piling them on his table, trying to build a pyramid. He must have known it settled me. Knows it still does.

Even though my racing heart has slowed, my hands still shake. It takes me several attempts to roll my first cigarette. It's not until I've rolled my fifth that the trembling subsides and I can speak.

"Aunt Celia had a stroke. Her brain's dead. They've got her hooked up to machines, but she's gone."

He's still for a long time then gives me a lopsided grin. His rollie defies gravity, as though it's stuck to the corner of his mouth with glue. I don't need to hear his deep rumbling voice to feel comforted.

I smile back. "I get to turn her off."

I can tell he's pleased by his slow nod as he sucks on his cigarette.

His implicit understanding floods me with relief. The warm air and hum of insects cocoon our silence. The rollie burns down between his fingers, a long dangle of ash curling at the end. Eventually he stubs it out on the concrete step and looks at me sideways.

I notice the heaviness in my limbs and the fog filling my head. I've had nothing more than stolen snatches of sleep for days. I yawn and use his shoulder to push myself to standing. He's always felt solid and reassuring.

"Reckon it's time to turn in. Night, Pa."

In the cabin I collapse onto the long vinyl seat against the wall. I'm so tired that the hard-edged splits in the cover don't bother me. I don't care that the pillow is dotted with mildew. I'm out.

Day arrives like syrup, thick and hot. Humidity clings to everything, leaving my skin slick with grime. A fine dribble of saliva slides down my chin. I wipe it off and sit up.

Groggy from too little sleep, it takes me a while to work out where I am. I'm inside the old site cabin above the quarry. Through the gaping hole in the roof I see a canopy of green so dark it looks black, and beyond that a solid blue sky. Vines snake their way in and cover one of the walls and what's left of the furniture. Every surface is covered in graffiti. There's a scorch mark on the floor and up the wall where someone's lit a fire.

Pa...

In my tiredness he seemed so real, but I know he's been dead for years.

I cradle my head in my hands and his death hits me again – a punch in the guts.

Then I remember Aunt Celia in hospital. How she found me last night.

I stumble out into bright light, the sun already high, squinting against the glare. I don't know what to do, where to go so she won't find me again. I try to shake the thoughts away. Maybe if I keep moving...

I stop at the top of the quarry. Below, at the water's edge, two men and a woman in khaki are unpacking equipment. My pulse quickens.

It's not unusual for people to visit the quarry. Families have picnics and go swimming. Teenagers make out after dark. Solitary walkers look into its depths, contemplating life and death. But these people aren't locals.

Anxiety sparks, growing like hunger once acknowledged. I take a deep breath and try to focus on what they're doing. The men pick up a large metal storage box and carry it into the vegetation. The woman's connecting wires from what looks like a boom mic to a computer. A thought emerges. They're here for the noise. The memory of its pounding still throbs, a physical sensation in my ears.

The woman finishes what she's doing, then stands on the quarry's edge with hands on hips, looking at the cliff. She glances up and sees me, then points at the path, at herself, then at me. She wants to come up.

I don't want to talk to her. I want to run back through the trees and hide in the cabin but I'm paralysed. My feet won't obey me and my mouth can't form the words to tell her to stay where she is.

She climbs the path quickly and approaches me, holding out her hand. "Hi, I'm Dr Oberon."

I thrust out my hand on autopilot. Her grip is calloused and firm.

"From the uni's spelaeology department."

I still can't speak.

"I study caves." She smiles, raising her eyebrows as though she's waiting for something.

My skin itches. I don't like the way she's staring at me. As though she knows.

"And you are…?"

"Um… Nell. Nell Brewster."

She looks around. "What are you doing up here?"

Why is she asking that? I scratch the back of my neck. My nails ignite the rest of my skin into an angry blaze. "Nothing." It sounds pathetic. "Ah… I just like it up here. It reminds me of my grandfather." I flail a hand in the direction of the cabin.

She looks into the thick vegetation, but from here she won't see through the tangle of vines and trees.

"My colleagues and I are here to investigate the noise."

My stomach turns over, sending bile up into my throat.

"Have you heard it?"

I cross my arms. I want her to stop. I kick at the dirt.

She shifts from foot to foot. "Some of the locals have described it as a thudding sound, like a… like a drum?" I remain silent. A tiny frown appears on her forehead. "Maybe you know when it started?"

I remember the exact moment the noise started. Celia screaming, hitting, darkness filling my head. "No." The lie catches in my throat, its sourness pressing my lips into a thin line.

"Ah… how often does it occur? Every day?"

I shrug.

She looks frustrated.

I've won, I know I've won. But the thought crushes me. It's exactly how Celia behaves, engaging in conflict, relishing petty victories imagined or real. I drop my arms. "It doesn't happen every day, but most. It's loud. Echoes off the cliffs. It sounds…" A shiver runs through me, cold and sharp. "Like a beating heart." I rush the words out.

She frowns, as though that's not what she was expecting to hear, but she's looking down.

I'm gripping her arm. I let go. My nails have left small crescents in her skin.

I want to tell her it's not me… that it can't be me.

She leans away and speaks quickly, clipping her words. "Beating. Makes sense. There's a network of caves below the island. They're filled with water. We think it's the tides. When the swell's just right. A bit like water-hammer in a pipe."

Does she really believe water can make a noise like that?

I don't want to answer any more questions.

"Sorry. I have to go." I leave her with her hands dangling at her sides, her mouth open.

The weight of the sun makes my shoulders sag. The walk back to town leaves me covered in sweat.

My aunt's house is a two-bedroom fibro shack. Dark green paint flakes off the outside, revealing pink and duck egg blue beneath. The garden is a mess of knee-high weeds. It's not really her house. It belonged to Pa, but everyone else has left or died. Now I guess it's mine.

The flyscreen door screeches open, bangs closed behind me. Inside it's dark. Mould spots the walls. The lino's cracked and curling. The ceiling is yellowed from decades of cigarette smoke. Dirty net curtains hang over the windows.

The kitchen's filled with rubbish. I kick through empty bottles and plastic wrappers. Open tins sit on the bench, their unfinished contents stinking and furry. The smell sticks in my throat and makes me gag. Anger fills me. I want to rid the house of my aunt's existence, obliterate all traces of her. I drag the bin inside, scoop up armfuls of refuse and throw them at it, smashing bottles as glass collides with glass. When I'm done the kitchen still feels full of my aunt's presence.

My chest heaves and I'm sobbing, great big juddering cries that tear at my throat. I cry for my mum. I cry for the little girl Celia beat out of me.

Then I hear it. It's faint but growing louder. Celia's found me again. Maybe she didn't like me cleaning out her shit. She fills me with noise, low and deep, throbbing slowly.

"Leave me alone, you bitch!" I cry, putting my hands over my ears.

The noise just gets louder.

I crawl under the table and curl into a ball, whispering, "Please, please, please…" but it doesn't help. She won't stop. She'll never stop.

I shut my eyes. The noise gets louder. I can't move. Time slips around me, over me, through me, stretching until I don't know where I am. I'm not asleep but I'm not awake either.

Awareness returns in a rush.

I'm on the floor, every vertebra aching. The house is quiet save for the ticking of the corrugated iron roof as it cools. I crawl out from beneath the table. The sun is low on the horizon and there's a heaviness in the air that signals a storm.

Then I remember. Celia's lying in hospital, brain dead, but alive. She can still get at me because I haven't turned her off yet.

And in that moment I know what I need to do and when I'm going to do it. I look at the time. I shower and dress, then make the last ferry to the mainland with a few minutes to spare.

Standing at the stern, I watch as the island recedes, a mass of dark clouds gathering behind it. Then the storm's moving towards me, swallowing the island, a towering mountain.

It's Celia. She's angry I've left.

The first hint of cool air pushes my hair back. It's smells like her, pungent and sharp. I face her head on, watching her anger flash inside the clouds, lighting them up from within.

She's trying to stop me but there's nothing she can do now. Heavy drops of rain pelt my skin like splintered glass. I don't care what she does. I'm going to turn her off and watch as she takes her last breath. Watch as her pulse flickers in her neck then stills. Leave her eyes open to stare at nothing forever. She's edging closer but she's too late. We berth and I'm running through the rain, lightning crashing around me, then I'm inside the hospital. Celia rages at the door, smashing and thundering. Impotent.

I point a finger at her. "See this?" I turn my finger around, marvelling at it. "This is your end." I turn and run.

The same nurse greets me in the ICU. "Get caught in the rain love? You look a mess."

I drip on the floor. "I've made my decision."

She looks at me, suddenly wary. She reaches out to pat me, but drops her hand. "I'll get the paperwork in order."

I nod and the nurse leaves the room.

I stand over Celia. She looks brittle and pale but I know what she's capable of, even now. I lean in close, my lips right next to her ear.

"You're fucked. I'm going to kill you."

For the next hour I sit rigidly still as the storm rages on and watch the ventilator inflating her lungs. I imagine it filling her with poisonous gas instead of air. I drink a watery, sugary tea the nurse brings me. A doctor arrives and talks at me about what to expect when the life support systems are turned off. I listen intently as she explains Celia's too weak to keep breathing on her own; how her heart will slow and stop. I bite my cheek in excitement. Blood coats my tongue, releasing a rusty tang.

Outside the storm subsides. Celia knows she's failing.

I start my countdown. My eyes flick to the clock on the wall every few seconds.

And then it's time. I know there are other people in the room, but I don't look at them. I just stand, walk over to the machines, and turn off the power. The ventilator stops its repetitive shushing. The heart monitor slows, then stops, flatlining.

The doctor checks her watch. "Time of death, twelve am."

Everything is quiet. No beeping, no ventilator wheeze. No rain or thunder, the storm is spent. No low, resonant beating in my head. No noise. She's dead. I could sing.

Midnight is my favourite time.

Kylie Pfeiffer is an author who writes for older children, adults, and anyone in between. She loves to entertain her readers, but also wants to make them think. She has co-authored three award-winning teen fiction books, 'A Dolphin for Naia', 'Rider & the Hummingbird', and 'The Time of the jade Spider'. Kylie is currently working on a number of independent and collaborative writing projects.

And the distant dark past...

Finding Jenna

Renee Jones

Lucy sat hunched over her desk, drumming her fingers as she scanned the papers in the lamp light. The clock beside her flashed 1am. She thumbed through a notebook filled with her best friend Jenna's handwriting, looking for clues. It had been only a week since Lucy's uncle took Jenna out on a geological research expedition and never returned.

She looked up as another guttural moan floated on the hot breeze through her open window. No wonder tourists are leaving the island in droves, she thought, before her mind went back to the missing pair. "Do you know where they are?" she asked the noise as she concentrated on the noise's notes and inflections, until it petered out. "Well, you're no help."

Lucy rubbed her eyes and focussed again on the papers and notebooks from the cardboard box David had dropped around earlier, spread across the desk like a puzzle waiting to be solved.

"You're an investigative journalist Lucy," he'd said, shoving the box into her arms. "You'll find an answer and you'll find my wife. There's got to be something here." His eyes were red and puffy. She pushed the memory away.

"Where are you, Jenna?" she asked the open notebook. "Everything you wrote was so meticulous. David's right – you must have at least left us clues." Lucy turned over the page to a hasty sketch of the quarry, notes about her uncle's advice on explosions, and some strange scribbles. Her eyes darted over the page; she recognised the peculiar forms and swirls. The realisation started as a niggling feeling in the back of her mind – an old memory working past the worry, tiredness, and concern – then finally floated to the surface. It was their secret written language from their youth!

"Oh," she silently mouthed as she deciphered the text, excitement and hope dancing in her mind.

Bang 15 – opened door to a new cave. Will explore tomorrow. Might find rocks been looking for!

Lucy stared at the message and looked back at the X marked next to the text on the quarry wall sketch. She fumbled around the papers on her desk for her phone and messaged David.

Have found a promising clue… looks like Uncle's explosion opened a cave none of us knew about and they may have gone exploring. Meet me at Minna's shop at 8am to investigate?

The phone vibrated immediately in her hand with a reply.

David: *Meet earlier!!!*

Can't. Have to wait til parents leave.

David: *OK. We need to get in quick, I heard at the centre that some investigation team is coming tomorrow arvo to check out quarry.*

K. See you then.

"Can't sleep Lucy?" a familiar voice asked from her doorway. She smiled and swivelled around to face her dad as he leaned on the door frame. He was dressed only in his bed shorts, his arms crossed against his broad chest. Another guttural moan drifted into the room. "The heat's bad enough but that sound doesn't help. It's creepy," she replied.

"Yes, well, you should have stayed on the mainland 'til this was sorted out," he said, walking over to the bed and sitting down on the edge closest to her, "where it's safe."

"I couldn't stay away. Not with Jenna and Uncle missing." She shrugged and leaned back in her chair. "Where do you think they are?" He had been his usual silent self since she arrived, but she'd never known him to be up this late or unable to sleep.

He sighed. "We've explored everywhere, it's like they've vanished."

Lucy wheeled her chair closer to him and put her feet up on the bed beside him. "People don't just vanish."

"I guess there's a first time for everything." He looked down at his palms in his lap. "I had no concerns about him going down with Jenna to the quarry to help out. It was for research. And Simon was so proud of his only daughter winning that grant. As any father would be. But your uncle was the best explosives man in mining. He kept his skills up. I can't imagine him blowing them both up."

Lucy gasped. "Is that what you think?"

"No, not me, I've heard whispers, but nothing to my face." They sat in silence for a minute. "Natives from the other islands have been leaving their jobs too and heading back, which is not like them at all."

"Really?" She pushed aside thoughts of accidental explosions. "Why?"

"They believe the groans and sightings are signs of some mythical goddess trapped here thousands of years ago. It could be the other rumours scaring them away as well."

Lucy waited quietly before prompting him. "What other rumours?"

"They're saying some tourist might have killed them, that there's a murderer loose on the island. It is strange though that it happened so soon after the explosion."

"Do any tourists think there's a murderer lurking around?" she asked, with her eyebrows raised.

He scoffed. "They're blaming the sightings and things going missing on us locals! And once a rumour like that starts it sticks like mud. Like the animal sightings. Now *there's* a rumour that has grown legs and taken a life of its own. We have no wild animals on the island. I mean, someone might have brought in a dog or something, but surely we would have seen it during the day."

Lucy nodded, chewing her lip and mentally sorting through the facts. "I just want to know, Dad, there has to be some hard evidence around this, something to tell us what happened."

"I know," he tutted. "You always need to keep going until you find the answer."

Another moan twisted through the window and snuffed out their conversation.

He slapped his hands on his knees and stood up. "Well, at least we will have answers starting tomorrow. I'm picking up Simon in the morning. He's determined to know what's happened to Jenna. And the investigation team is coming from the mainland. You should be able to get your answers from them." He looked her square in the eye. "I want you to stay away from the quarry, Lucy. I know you will be wanting to go down there. But until we know what's going on, it's not safe to be wandering around. We've even had to put guns in the carts, otherwise staff wouldn't deliver room service. You need to stay here and work through all this paperwork for the investigation team. Plus, by the feel of this heat, a big storm is on its way later."

"Okay." She mentally crossed her fingers behind her back. "Night, Dad."

He kissed the top of her head.

When he left the room, she turned back to the notebook.

———

Lucy swigged on the last of her water as beads of sweat dripped down her face and back. The heat was even more oppressive in the daytime. The walk to the only shop wasn't long and, as she neared it, she spotted David standing out the front waiting.

"Hey, I was starting to think you weren't going to show," he said, tapping his foot.

She hugged him. "I know, I had to wait for my parents to leave." She stepped past him. "I just need to duck in and grab some more water. This heat is killing me."

"Hurry," he called after her, lifting his backpack from where it had been at his feet.

As she walked into the lightly air-conditioned shop, she called out to the new faces behind the counter. "Morning, Minna, Roj!"

Still setting up, the couple smiled and waved back at her. Lucy would never understand how anyone would want to move from the mainland, after having worked in a university, to an island as isolated as this. There seemed to be more to that story, but she filed it away for another day.

In front of the water fridge at the back of the shop were two young people dressed in casual summer clothes. Tribal tattoos unique to the neighbouring island community adorned their muscular tanned arms. "Grab as much as you can carry and let's get off this damn island," the man hissed to the woman, who was staring blankly at the tins in her hands.

"I still can't believe the story is true," she said, her voice wavering slightly.

"I wouldn't have believed it if I didn't see it with my own eyes." The man patted her arm.

Lucy cleared her throat. "Sorry, I just need to grab a bottle of water from behind you guys." She gestured to the fridge.

They looked startled for a second before shuffling to one side.

"Thanks." She pulled a bottle out of the fridge. "You guys want one too?"

"Uh no, we're okay," the man said.

Lucy smiled at them and looked over to the woman who, on closer inspection, might have been in her teens. "I couldn't help overhearing what you said. You saw something?" Lucy stepped closer. "Please, it's my family who's gone missing. I need to find the truth. Some things happening on this island are well out of place."

The man considered her for a moment. "Are you Matt's girl?"

"Yes, he's my dad." She let that hang between them.

"He's a good man, a good boss," the girl chimed in.

Lucy nodded. "So is my missing uncle."

The girl glanced at the man for a minute, who shrugged. She turned back to Lucy, her eyes wide. "We saw a monster," she said, "a beast that matches our elders' stories about demons guarding a jealous goddess."

"You saw a monster? Are you sure it wasn't a loose dog? Where did you see it?"

"Last night, on one of the pathways at the quarry, from the golf cart. We saw it on our way back from the campgrounds." Small beads of sweat started to line the girl's brow and the top of her lip, even though inside the shop was cool.

"What did it look like?"

"Half man, half monster. It walked on hind legs but was kind of hunched over. It was hard to see but it was black and looked like it was covered in fur. The most frightening part was the eyes. The red glowing eyes." The girl shuddered. "That noise started and it turned and ran the other way."

"Sounds like you were lucky!" Lucy exclaimed, wondering what it was they saw. Maybe a dog with rabies? Maybe someone snuck their dog onto the island and was letting it out at night? Or a clueless tourist taking a late night hike, it wasn't that uncommon.

"We're getting out of here as soon as we can," the girl added. "If the demons are free then Te-neti must be coming too, and we don't want to be around to deal with the vengeance of that goddess."

"Te-neti?"

"Yeah," the girl nodded, her eyes solemn and honest, "she's one of our creation gods. The way our elders tell it, Te-neti was one of three sisters who were responsible for bringing life to all the islands. But Te-neti was also jealous and wanted to be the most powerful. She killed people to punish anyone who didn't love her. The other two sisters created this island as a prison to hold her and she has been here ever since, trapped in the rock. That's why no other island clans would come and work in the quarry when it was operational. They believed it was cursed."

"Or that disturbing the rock would somehow awaken Te-Neti," the man added.

"C'mon, Lucy," David called impatiently from the doorway, "we don't have all day."

"Good luck." The woman waved as her companion pulled her away.

"Do you think they were telling the truth?" David asked as they neared the base of the quarry wall. They both had sweat stains on their shirts, faces red from exertion and heat. Lucy had recounted the conversation from the shop as they had walked through the forest shortcut.

"Well, they saw something," Lucy said. She stopped walking, pulled out Jenna's notebook and opened it to the page with the sketch of the quarry. She held it up and turned it in front of her, trying to find the right angle and a more exact location. "If only one of them had seen it then I would have said probably not, but it's hard when you have two witnesses, in my experience anyway. But a monster, that's a bit of a stretch. There would be more evidence.

Interesting though, I didn't think the younger generation were that connected to the stories of their elders."

"I don't know what to believe at the moment, but I do have one of Simon's guns in my bag."

"What, why?"

"Don't worry, it's secure. There have been so many rumours I didn't want to take the chance. Plus your dad would be even angrier if he knew we came here unarmed."

Lucy nodded. "It's strange that we grew up so carefree and now we are carrying a gun. When we return with Jenna and Uncle, our sneaky investigation will be forgiven." She lined the drawing in the book up with the wall. "I think that's the entry point – up on that track. I'm not sure why she wanted samples from there, but I'm certain that's where they went in. It's hard to tell if there is an entrance or just wall." Lucy pulled out her phone and took a photograph.

"What's with that?"

"Huh?" she grunted at him.

"Why are you taking photos?"

"Hm, a professional habit, to document what we find, to review if we need to get our heads around anything." She turned to him and he nodded. "Let's go."

They turned towards the track and set off in their own thoughts. Gravel crunched under their shoes, the uneven quarry wall on their right. The area was deserted. The rest of the island were under a fan or air conditioning.

"Check this out," David called.

Lucy stopped. She turned to see him tracing something in the rock with his finger. She stepped towards him. Three slashes were gouged into the granite. "That's strange," she mumbled and pulled her phone out of her pocket. She snapped two shots, one with David's hand for a size reference. "Maybe it was from the explosion. I don't think we are far now."

They walked a little faster until they reached a person-sized hole a short distance along the rock face, connected to the track by a narrow ledge.

"How has everyone else missed this?" she exclaimed. They stared at the hole.

"I've been to the quarry a hundred times since they went missing and it's the first time I've seen it." He scratched his head through his hat.

"But we couldn't see it from the ground without Jenna's map. It's kind of like an optical illusion. There's another ledge further along too."

David started edging his way over to the hole.

Lucy followed, running her hand over the thick wall of the opening as she reached it. It was cold and almost black in colour, unlike the rest of the quarry – so unfamiliar in a place she had visited many times before. *How did Uncle even blast this entrance?* Lucy thought as she stepped through the hole. *It's high up and not easy to reach.*

The hole opened onto a sunlight-flooded chamber, sunbeams striking from another entrance higher up the inside wall, creating strong shafts of light as well as shadows. It was spacious and breezy, reminding her of the space under a Queenslander she had stayed in once. There was a supporting beam on the far side and rock formations littered the floor.

David stepped into the chamber and walked to the far end. The ceiling was high, and even with his arm stretched up he couldn't reach it. He swung his backpack off. "Grab your flashlight," he said, fishing his out of his backpack. "There's some light, but I think there are more chambers down the back here where the light doesn't reach."

Lucy snapped some photos of the entrance, then pulled her Maglite torch out of her bag, the weight heavy and comforting in her hand. She dropped her bag next to his on the floor and walked over to where David was examining the sunlit wall on the right-hand side of the chamber.

"There's more of those marks here, like someone's dragged something along the wall." David ran his fingers along the marks and turned back to the wider chamber.

"What would make a mark like that? It can't have been the explosion. Look at this room, it's too well sculpted," Lucy said. "Hand sculpted even?"

"I don't know. And check out this thing in the middle." David clicked on his torch.

Lucy did the same and followed him over to the waist-high dark grey rock formation sprouting out from the centre of the chamber. The centre of it glowed when they shone their torches on it. Lucy pulled out her phone and took a photo, then turned on its video mode, keeping the phone on and in her hand.

A deep wail echoed through the cave, loud and intense.

David jumped and Lucy's stomach leapt into her throat.

"Jenna?" David strode across the sunbeams and out of sight.

"Wait!" Lucy called after him. "We don't know who's here or who's making the noise," she hissed. "It could be that murderer everyone's been talking about." Only silence met her plea. Pushing her fear aside, Lucy reluctantly followed.

In the dark space were three passageways. David was standing in the middle one, shining his torch into the space beyond. His head was cocked, ear turned down the passage. "It's this one." His voice was a mixture of nerves and excitement. "She's down here, I know it." And before Lucy could say anything he disappeared again into the nothingness.

"Damn it," Lucy muttered, fighting every urge to run the other way, and propelling herself into the same tunnel.

David's heavy footsteps echoed through the stillness and she tried to keep in time with them. She could smell the air becoming thick and stale with a hint of decay, and she wondered momentarily if there were toxic gases in the cave. The sharp curves of the passageway made it hard for her to stay orientated. The soft edges of her torchlight caught strange symbols carved into the walls.

It wasn't long before the tight walls fell away to what appeared to be another chamber. The space wasn't much smaller than the other chambers. "There you are," she whispered under her breath when she saw David's outline in the shadow of his torchlight across the chamber. She moved towards to him, extending her phone and torch in front of her, anxious to be close to him again. There was something wrong about this place. David was still, his open mouth barely visible.

"What the…" escaped her lips as her eyes focused on the other shapes in the pool of David's yellow light.

In front of them, on a smooth rock altar raised half a meter off the ground were two anatomically correct human skeletons laid out. Beside the skull closest to them was a necklace, the heart pendant flush to the stone, a wedding ring and a small diamond ring.

Bile rose in Lucy's throat. Jenna's plain silver studs were there too. Lucy shone her torch on the other skeleton. Was that her uncle? She almost couldn't bear to look. "Where's your backpack David? Pass the gun."

"Huh?"

"You have the gun, remember. Pass it to me."

He felt his shoulders and looked at his feet. "I left it behind, in the other chamber."

"We have to go," she whispered, barely audible, her mouth so dry it was hard to form words. She moved the torch light around the chamber. More peculiar carved symbols adorned the walls and there was an elevated stone altar in the middle of the chamber. On the other side, she spotted the passage where they'd entered. Images of a serial killer or cannibal murderer flashed in her mind. She cursed herself for leaving the gun behind.

She turned back to David, his face wet as tears spilled from his eyes. He sniffed and a sob escaped. She put her arm around him and squeezed. "We have to go, for Jenna's sake," she gently cajoled him. "We have to make sure someone finds out and catches the sicko who did this. Someone will pay."

"I can't leave her." His voice was small.

"It won't be for long, we know where she is now and we'll come back." He nodded and she used her hand with the phone to guide him, keeping the torch extended in front of them.

A groan cut through the pitch black, filling the cave and bouncing around the walls, assaulting their ears, piercing their grief and stoking their fears.

For a moment they both froze, the torchlight wavering over the passage entrance; then Lucy nudged David towards it. In the darkness on her right, two red circles flashed through the heavy darkness. Lucy flicked her torchlight over, across the wall to where they were. *Eyes,* she thought, *someone's in here with us.*

The eyes were like specks, staring out from the wall.

David, watching the eyes, leaned into her, moving his arm to around her waist.

The wall eyes blinked and the space around them shook, little pieces of rock crumbling away. The crack of an outline formed in the wall around the eyes and spread down. Lucy trembled, unable to look away. The outline followed the familiar shape of a body. The rock between the cracks broke and fell away, much like a chick breaking the confines of its eggshell, revealing a muscular, animalistic body with dark skin, sprouted hair and fur: a beast breaking out of the wall. As the head finally freed from the wall, the roar that came from the beast's mouth was deafening, more dangerous and frightening than the moan.

Lucy could only watch as it pulled its claws and arms free from the wall.

"RUN!" David screamed.

Lucy turned to him, shocked and uncomprehending. Run where?

He jammed his hand into the small of her back and jerked her forward. "RUN RIGHT NOW!" he yelled.

The beast was almost free of the wall, its arms flailing as it pulled its legs free, its red eyes fixed on them.

Adrenalin whooshed through Lucy's veins, the flight response and the pressure of David's hand propelling her legs as they rushed into the passageway. She managed to keep the torchlight in front of them, pumping her legs, her fingers white as they gripped her phone, David's panting breath on her neck. They skidded and jerked around corners in the windy passage until finally, as they exited the corridor, Lucy tripped and went sprawling across the dark cave, the wind knocked out of her, skin scraping on the harsh uneven surface. Somehow she kept her grip on the phone, though her torch rolled away.

David stumbled over her, managed to stay upright and swung back round to her. "GET UP," he bellowed and was over her, his powerful arms hooked under hers as he pulled her to her feet. Blood oozed out of the fresh wounds on her chin, elbows, hands and knees. It didn't matter, only getting out of the chamber did.

The beast exploded from the passageway in a powerful blur of sharp teeth, red eyes, black fur and muscly limbs, and straight into David. The pair skidded into the back corner of the chamber, the beast gripping David in its strong arms. In one swift movement the beast slashed David's neck, removing his head from his body. Dark red blood squirted through the air. His body went limp, but the shock remained on his face as his head rolled past Lucy.

She opened her mouth in a silent scream.

The beast buried his teeth into the open wound, tearing at the flesh and guzzling the blood.

Another bolt of adrenaline shot through Lucy and she leapt from her spot, focused only on the opening out of this tomb. *I've got to survive, I have to warn everyone,* she screamed into her mind, sprinting towards the entrance.

Behind her, the sickening thud of David's body was followed by the rapid clicks of claws on rock and a sudden whimpering.

She twisted back around mid-stride. The beast was now wrapped around the glowing rock formation in the chamber's centre, a dark fluid dripping from a wound on his head, David's backpack twisted around one of his legs. Lucy sped towards the entrance, shot herself out into the bright sunlight, skidded on the loose gravel of the ledge, regained her balance and ran along it onto the track.

When she was halfway down the pathway, the beast roared and she knew it was out of the hole. A sob built in her throat. Pure fear spurred her on, her chest burning and muscles ready to snap.

From somewhere lower down, gunshots rang out.

Lucy searched frantically as she ran to see where they came from, trying to keep herself out of the line of fire. The gunshots kept sounding.

As she ran lower on the path, she spotted two men below, guns aimed back up the path. She looked over her shoulder to see the beast had stopped running. More shots were hitting its arms, legs and torso.

With renewed hope, she picked up her pace and reached the bottom of the track, then raced across the flat ground towards safety. Parked not far from the base was one of the carts from the camping grounds, her dad standing with a gun on his shoulder, aimed at the beast. Not far from him was Jenna's dad, Simon, reloading his gun then aiming it at the beast too.

"Help!" she yelled, making a beeline for them.

From the path the beast screamed, wounded and in pain.

With only meters to cover between them, she watched her dad click the safety on his gun, place it on the floor of the cart and stride towards her arms wide.

"Run Lucy, RUN!" he called. Simon and his gun remained trained on the beast.

She kept going and fell into his open arms. He held her upright and took in her dirty face, cuts and bruises.

"It's retreating, back to that spot you came out of!" Simon called.

"What are you doing here, Lucy?" her dad scolded. "I picked up Simon, brought him to see you but you weren't home. We called around and Minna said you went off somewhere with David. I knew you couldn't stay away."

She could barely see through the tears rolling down her cheeks. "It got David, and it got Jenna and Uncle," she sobbed. "They're all dead, they're all dead."

"WHAT?" Dad and Simon shouted in unison.

"We have to go in there," Simon said, gun in hand as he started towards the quarry path. "I've got to get Jenna."

"NO!" Lucy called, stopping him in his tracks. "It's too late. We have to get more help, more than just us." She scrambled into the back of the cart, sniffing back the tears, a laser focus taking over. "Hurry, hurry," she called.

"What do you want to do mate?" Dad asked, jumping into the driver's seat.

Simon looked at Lucy, his expression pleading. "I can't leave Jenna."

Lucy stared at him, the haunting image of Jenna's skeleton laid out fresh in her mind. *David 'had' to get Jenna and look what happened to him,* she thought and shuddered. "There's nothing left of Jenna, I'm sorry," she said.

"But the beast is injured now." Simon gestured to the chamber's entrance, his face crumpling under the news of his beloved daughter. "We can finish it off."

"Please, Simon, trust me," Lucy begged. "If you love Jenna, you will make sure we get out of here now and meet the investigators when they arrive." Blood kept oozing from her chin and other wounds. All she wanted was to put as much distance as she could between them and the monster, the smell of David's blood fresh in her nostrils and the vision of his head rolling past her. "Please

Simon, I can't lose anyone else, I couldn't bear it." She looked him in the eye. "I need you to come with us. Now."

His shoulders slumped. Without another word, he got into the cart and secured his gun. He buried his face in his hands, his elbows on his knees to prop him up. The cart started, and her dad spun the wheel, put his foot down and they sped away.

Silent tears rolled down Lucy's cheeks as the forest whipped past them.

"At least we got some shots in," her dad said to no one in particular, "wounded whatever that was, whatever's been causing that awful noise these past few weeks."

"No." Lucy was unable to keep the terror from her voice, "that monster had a terrible roar, but it sounded nothing like the island's noise."

"But if that beast hasn't been causing all that noise, what has?" he asked.

"For once, I don't want to find out," was all Lucy could say.

Renee Jones is a writer and communications specialist in the community services sector. Her love of the supernatural, fantasy and science fiction with a healthy dose of action influence her creative writing projects. While her days are spent creating compelling narratives for organisations and people with a disability, her spare time is spent traversing her imagination, meeting new characters and finding exciting ways to bring their stories into the written word. You will also find her interviews with pop culture authors, artists and creators online.

Then we cared about the future...

Guarding Temperance

Zena Shapter

The boom is so loud it jumps me out of my sleep, sends my heart fluttering so fast it's as if it wants to soar out of my chest and join the tension building in the soupy night air. I stare at the ceiling beams above me and wait, knowing what will follow. No rumbles. No reverberations. No flashes across a distant ocean's horizon. Because this is not a brewing thunderstorm. It's not even the island's rainy season. The boom simply resonates for a moment, demanding the attention of everyone on the island, then whistles like wind whooshing through treetops, speeds up and boils into a searing screech that forces me to clasp hands over ears and scrunch eyes up tight.

It's been the same every night now for weeks. The sooner they find out what's causing it the better. Tectonic plates rubbing? Some climate change phenomenon? A cart stuck torturing the old quarry's rail line? If I were in the army, like I wanted to be, I might be part of the military team arriving today to investigate. But I'm not, so I can't.

Once I'm certain the noise has stopped and the ringing in my head is after effects, I roll over and nuzzle into the cool edge of my pillow. The feel of it naturally brings thoughts of Matius to mind, and how I wish he were here. Since he arrived on the island, a month or so ago, we've spent so much time together – talking of our passion for the environment, our appreciation for biodiversity, how short-sighted humans can be when it comes to the planet and how much we want to change that. I thought he and I were at the very least friends. Clearly not, given the way he turned me down last night in front of everyone at Monday Trivia. No 'friend' would ever act like that.

I expect to relive the humiliation as I drift back to sleep but instead remember Alice chuckling and saying I deserved it. In my imagination I turn to her and ask how she'd know. Oh, that's right, I say to those I'm serving at the bar, Alice is the island's love guru. Never been with a man, lives with the only other spinster on the island, too scared to leave to find a love of her own, yet knows all about it from Mills and Boon. I launch into a hurtful tirade I'd never say in real life – I'm eloquent and people agree with me – then slip into an illusory self-satisfied sleep that cradles me until my morning alarm. Guilt finds me there.

Island life thrives off restraint, temperance, even in thought. Intolerance begets enemies. In a small community like ours, even a single enemy can make life hell.

I suppose that's why Alice reined herself in last night, after she'd gone too far with her teasing. She dropped her usually generous Islander smile, her plump cheeks sagging into jowls with it, and she reached across the bar to pat my hand sympathetically, like she was giving bad news to one of her patients. The short sleeve of her floral dress strained so tight across her chubby arm it surely cut off her circulation. "I'm sure he's got good reason, Joey," she consoled with a smile as tight as her sleeve. "People usually do."

"Not always," I mutter, sitting up in bed and rubbing my eyes. It's clearer to me now than ever: I need to get off this island, as soon as possible. "Hopefully tonight." This place is a dump and everyone knows it. Noise or no noise, I should've left years ago.

As I move around the bedroom, soft warm air glides around my bare shoulders like a bath, clean and fresh until I open my door and head towards the bathroom. In the hallway it's tart with stale beer, spilt wine and crushed peanuts. No matter how much I scrub around the bar, my shoes stick on its floorboards and the place reeks. Opening the windows each morning helps but not much.

I pause at the bathroom door. Didn't Alice say Mrs Beecher was coming to see her first thing? Mrs Beecher detests the smell of beer...

With a huff I hurry into the communal hall that doubles during the day as Alice's consulting rooms, and slide open every window with a yank. The movement twangs my bad shoulder, even though Alice said it shouldn't hurt after a year. It's been five.

When I get a job on the mainland I'll go see a specialist.

Opposite the bar area, I fling open the door that leads onto the centre's deck, wooden picnic tables surrounded by a forest of palms, ferns and orchids that tumble down towards the azure waters of Amama Harbour. I pause to farewell the view, because hopefully I'll be leaving tonight, then spy a figure in a pale uniform trudging up the Cove Road.

Officer Hartono has arranged for a professional team to come from the mainland today and investigate the boom noise – geologists, scientists, military, I'm unsure who exactly – but this figure is solitary. As he hikes up the hill and passes under leafy palm trees and house verandahs, the sun doesn't glare as harshly on him and I can make out the khaki colour of Matius's shorts and shirt, his wide-brimmed ranger hat and bulky canvas backpack, the awkward stride of someone who still doesn't know what they're doing here or why. The way he holds himself is almost apologetic, like he knows he's too good for this place but doesn't want others to feel bad that they aren't. With that kind of restraint, it's no surprise he's become popular here.

I step onto the deck to watch him, tilt my head and glide my hair over a shoulder to leave the other exposed like an invitation. A breeze filled with hibiscus and frangipani plays with some strands close to my waist. Sunlight gleams on my skin, gentle as it is this time of day, and I hope Matius sees me gazing across the ocean… until I realise I'm still in my nightdress. It's white and thin and the sun's probably shining all the way through it.

I back into the communal hall and bang into tables and chairs to reach the door that fronts onto Cove Road. A glass panel in its top section gives me a limited view of the hill. When Matius strides into view, I can't take my eyes off him. His skin is the brown of tropical sun, smooth like gliding in warm ocean currents, tense like red crab pincers waiting to snap. Faded tattoo lines swirl across his face, reaching past his ears and disappearing into short black hair – shadows of tribal ink. Each eyebrow is trimmed at the ends into sections. Lips the colour of a sunset's last rays tighten to match the urgency in his eyes, which dart left and right as he hurries along, like he either doesn't want to be seen or needs to know who sees him. So it's no surprise he spots me behind the community centre door.

For a moment his eyes are both bright and dark, alive with a fire that sees me as oxygen it needs to consume, yet shadowed by a regret for that consumption. Then he frowns and scrunches up his eyes like he's annoyed with my presence. I don't understand. The way he acts around me clearly indicates interest. The way we talk for hours backs that up. What I feel for him backs that up. Yet our interactions always end like this: on a moment of infuriation. And when I finally invited him on a date last night, he declined with an exasperation that implied to everyone it wasn't the first time I'd asked. As if a girl like me needed to ask any man twice.

I tut and spin around as if insulted by his expression, then storm back into the centre's living quarters and the bathroom. I have more important things to be doing than worrying about Matius. If my Skype interview this afternoon goes well, I'll be able to start a new life, catch a boat to the mainland with whoever on Hartono's team isn't staying the night, and start saving the environment my own way, with Greenworld. It should go well. My final exam marks were impressive; my published articles on island restoration in the Pacific more so – Dad's journalist contacts helped ensure that. I'm missing deep ocean sailing experience but Granddad dying explains why I couldn't leave the island to get some. Greenworld should know that's why I need them, why I'll accept a lower salary than other activists they might be considering, and if they don't know I'll tell them at five o'clock this afternoon via Skype, provided the connection doesn't drop out as it has been lately.

There's nothing I can do about that of course. I can only do what I can to be ready, look the part and hope it's enough. I plait my long hair into a braid, notice my gold nose ring and wonder if I should take it out for the interview. Mum always hated facial piercings.

"Makes women look like whores," she snapped when I asked to get one.

In hindsight my timing was probably wrong. It was right before her last deployment, right after she'd shaved her head ready for active duty. I was fifteen and used to her going away. How was I supposed to know that time she wouldn't come back?

"What do you care? You're never here," I snapped back.

In truth she was 'there' more than regular working mums – we lived a block outside the base so she got home most nights at five thirty-five precisely.

"Get your nose pierced," she told me, "and they'll never accept you."

"This is the twenty-first century, Mum." I wanted to be a combat engineer, later an architectural draughtsman – fight for my country as she did. "The Army's more progressive than the air force."

"I meant your future squadron. Look like you want to be treated, Joey."

"I should've asked Dad." I knew that would hurt her.

It ended up hurting me more: those were the last words I ever said to her. A week later our lives changed forever. If she hadn't died, Dad wouldn't have moved back here to the island, I wouldn't have had to train for my pre-entry fitness assessment on these rocky slopes, and I wouldn't have come off that boulder on my mountain bike, fallen funny, broken my collarbone and damaged my shoulder. While the army would have accepted an application by a keen and healthy seventeen-year-old, they had no choice but to reject mine on the basis of my newly limited mobility.

That's when I got my nose ring – a symbol of new dreams and ambitions: to save my country in a different way, with an environmental protection and conservation degree. I would have given my life for my country by serving in the military, as Mum did. With a career as an activist, there was a chance I still could. Is.

The nose ring stays.

"Joey?" The Cove Road door squeaks open and Alice's humble footsteps shuffle inside. "I'm here!" she calls. "Oh, you opened up the windows. Good, good. That will be better for Mrs Beecher. Did you speak to Angel about the flyscreen?"

"Three days ago."

"That's my girl, saving the world already – first: mosquitoes; next: climate change and pollution."

"The planet won't heal itself."

"As long as you stay happy *and* safe."

She's referring to my Greenworld application. Activists have to be prepared to get hurt sometimes. What's one life, though, compared to the hundreds of species becoming extinct every day?

"What about the pig?" she asks.

"He said he'd start roasting it this morning." Though I have no idea why we're treating today like a holiday. "Reckon I can smell the fire already."

She sniffs. "Yeah, you could be right there. Good, good."

Back in my bedroom I pull on a shirt and shorts for my morning ride. My army-inspired fitness routine is still in place.

In the hall Alice pulls together tables and fills up the kettle. Her appointments can last over an hour. People often use them more as cake and coffee catch ups rather than for actual medical needs. It's a wonder Alice encourages it. Doesn't she want a life for herself?

"Your dad coming down later to report on things?" she calls out while I'm shovelling down some cereal.

"He's volunteered to sail some marine biologist around the island when they get here, something to do with the noise and crabs. Reckons he'll talk to the other specialists tonight."

"Good, good. Mainlanders will want to know what's happening. Didn't he interview OHar's father before he died?" She means Officer Hartono's father – a consultant Stoneco hired to assess our quarry and prevent it from falling into disuse. It took so long the family ended up staying. "They wrote an article together, didn't they, about the quarry affecting the island's stability?"

I join her in the hall, carrying my bowl. "Stability, you actually believe that? The quarry wasn't in use long enough to affect anything."

Alice is tipping a packet of biscuits onto a plate. "Why do you think it was closed then?"

I shrug. "Too expensive to transport stone back to the mainland? Too expensive to expand housing for the miners? Too expensive to risk boats anywhere along the coast, apart from the Cove? Everyone knows not to try landing anywhere else because of the winds. Too expensive to turn the Cove into a proper harbour that might…"

"Okay, okay, I get the idea."

"Dad wrote what he wrote to sell his work, that's what he does."

"You know my girl, if you stayed here," she cocks her head in thought, "you could work out how to fix all those things – make us thrive again."

"Did we ever?"

"We could even get some of those sun panels installed, for electricity. Your dad will miss you if you go – you're all he has left, you know that don't you, Joey?"

I glare at her then take my empty bowl into the kitchen.

"Sorry, Joey. It's just… we'll all miss you. Why not be an activist here, activate some of us?" She chuckles. "You shouldn't feel like you have to leave just because you've a degree now."

"I don't," I call back.

"Your mother would be as proud of you if you stayed. I hate seeing you so conflicted," she mutters to herself as if knowing I won't respond.

I don't because what would she know of my mum?

I rinse out my bowl and leave it in the sink for later. Right now I've got no study to do – no text books, Skype classes or assignments – just fresh air and solitude to enjoy, peace and quiet until lunchtime when I have to be back to serve drinks to OHar's mainland team.

"See you, Alice!" I shout from the backdoor, grabbing my water bottle.

She calls out some kind of farewell.

I close the door, wheel my bike away from the lean-to and onto the road, snap my bottle into its holder, then push all thoughts of Alice and Matius away, and pedal uphill like I'm fighting a tidal wave determined to drown and keep me here until I wither away and die as miserably as everyone else. I don't want Monday Trivia to be the highlight of my week. I don't want to settle down and marry Deacon or Tane. When Dad asks me what I want to do for my birthday, I want to be full of ideas, not unable to think of a single thing I want to do here. I've scaled North Point and West Point countless times, ridden all through the jungle in between, been to the coral limestone reefs around South Point, through the thick forest near Steep Point and around the old quarry. White Beach and West White Beach both have transparent water, fine banks of sand, rugged green hills rising behind them. The whole island's beautiful but there's nothing more to do; nothing more to see. It might be enough for others, but I want to make a difference to the world. Greenworld needs people like me, people willing to risk their lives for the sake of the planet. I'm not needed on a tiny island in the middle of the Pacific Ocean.

At the base of Eastern Hill I pause to catch my breath, gaze back across Amama Harbour, and know this is how Mum must have felt when Dad brought her here to marry. I wish she were here to talk to, even if only to tell me to take my nose ring out.

Maybe I will later.

I angle my handlebars down old Quarry Road, push off and glide west, braking until I reach the waterfall track. There I let go, lean left and take the track, not that I'm going to the waterfall. Maybe Steep Point, again, or down through Lofty Hill, again.

When the gradient levels I pedal fast, ducking under branches and changing gears as the ground slopes up or down. My thigh muscles burn after the fourth incline, though not as much as they will pumping up Quarry Road later.

I head towards the coast, lose myself in a rhythm of pedalling and gliding, not as fast as I used to before I broke my collarbone, but fast enough. I don't stop again until the track splits east and west. A thick gust blowing towards Steep Point tempts me to follow it, so I don't have to ride into a headwind. At the same time the west track across Lofty Hill is shaded by trees and the sun's already heaving through the canopy. I back into the shade so my skin doesn't blister like Angel's roasting pig, and gulp down some water. When I lower my head I notice a movement in the trees.

No, not in the trees – beyond them. On the downside of Lofty Hill, Matius is weaving his way through the scrub, heading for the quarry.

Through the scrub? Why hasn't he walked down Quarry Road? If he's making preparations ahead of Hartono's team, wouldn't he do them down on the quarry floor? He couldn't be lost – he's been surveying the island for the entire time he's been here, at least that's what everyone says. Perhaps he's doing some conservation work… on the one day top scientists are coming to look at the place?

I clack my bottle away, then angle my front wheel down the west track and glide silently after him. Ferns whack against my shins. Humps and pebbles judder my handlebars. Wind blasts my eyes into a squint. He disappears out of sight. I brake and release until I'm sailing around a bend that opens onto a ledge overlooking the quarry. I stop behind a small palm tree, its fronds snap-dry and sharp. From here a dirt track winds around the grey quarry top before curling down the far slope of scrub, levelling with the quarry floor and hugging its lake before joining the Quarry Road. There's no sign of Matius anywhere – not on the track, in the thicket of trees entwined alongside it, or among the slabs and slates of rubble below. The place smells of dust and little else.

I lean my bike against the palm trunk and, thighs shaking, creep towards the edge.

A pebble splashes into the lake below, though not from me. Its drop echoes around the hollow.

I peer over.

The sheer-cut sides of the quarry plunge, drab and scarred from diggers' teeth, straight into deep aqua water – completely mirror-still apart from slight ripples of disturbance a short distance away. They reach the rockface below, refract against grass clumps sprouting at the base, then undulate out towards the reflection of a figure clinging to the rock, their khaki outfit blending between striations of orange and white in the stone. I go to call out but stop when Matius disappears from the reflection. I drop to my knees and lean further over the edge. Beneath me is a narrow ledge that slopes towards a shaft of broken rock, and a dark depression behind it.

A cave?

"Matius?" I call out.

No answer.

The ledge is narrow enough to be invisible from lower down, yet wide enough for both my feet. I turn and lower myself onto it, keeping a firm grip on the rockface as I ease myself along. I'll probably be doing much more dangerous things for Greenworld.

Fine by me.

The closer I get to the broken rock the more it appears to hide an entrance, about Matius's height and width. The ledge corners into it, then a cool blackness consumes the space. I listen, straining to hear something other than wind rustling through trees or the distant chatter of frigate birds. But when I take a deep breath and smell electrical equipment, I dive sideways into the black. Matius went in here. So I can go in here.

I use my foot as a guide, feeling for the solid rock in front of me while keeping my hands on the snug stonewalls closing in. Soon a pale light gives eerie form to a chiselled passageway… and downward steps. Cut into the walls at hip height is a horizontal groove, so smooth and consistent it acts like a handrail. I creep down, holding on and listening. There's nothing for five minutes, ten minutes – I'm about to turn back when the light grows stronger and develops an unnatural luminosity. I keep going, down and down, for so long I must be level with the quarry floor.

Distant footsteps slap across flat ground and something metallic scrapes. The steps finish and become a path. I keep my hands on the walls and tiptoe closer. More scraping. A metal tool tinkles to the ground. Matius swears. The wall on my right side turns into a bumpy rockfall of boulders and stone. Sunlight gleams through chinks and I realise where I am: on the far side of the quarry lake where a dark rocky hollow dips into the rock. I assumed it was the remnants of some blast site, now disused and inaccessible because of the lake. In the rainy season lake water swells and floods through here.

Matius swears again and throws something. I round a bend and see him sitting on the floor of a large but low-ceilinged cave, surrounded by high tech equipment, bright spotlights and scattered tools. His hat and now-empty backpack are discarded nearby. What is all this? Metal cylinders as wide as fork-lift tyres stick upright from the floor to support a huge metallic-pink disc at head height. It reminds me of a 1950s UFO though it's made of alloys I don't recognise, its shell both liquid and solid at the same time – pink hues and silver highlights swirl under a shiny hard surface, like water currents rippling under the smooth skin of a still lake. Near Matius, a cut-out section is raised to reveal intricate mechanical workings and circuit boards with an interface like no computing device I've ever seen, all immersed in a pink gel that oozes over the side and drips onto the cave floor.

Matius mutters in a language I've never heard, then leans closer to the metal casing between his legs and turns a screwdriver into it with greater gusto. Pink gel covers his hands. Whatever he's doing, he looks stressed – no, panicked. He turns his screwdriver like the life of a loved one depends on his finishing.

"Matius?"

He looks up, his beautiful mouth agape, his eyes wide yet dim with shock as he struggles to react. Once he realises I'm actually there, a fire returns to them. His mouth closes into a firm purse. "What are you doing here?"

I cross my arms. "Same question right back at ya. What is all this?"

He looks around, decides something and visibly deflates. Whatever lie he was thinking of trying fades away like he doesn't have the energy for deception today. "I don't suppose you'd believe I'm here to save the world?"

Even defeated he entrances me. "Is this what's been making that boom noise?"

"What do you think?"

"I think there's no way you could get all this down here by yourself, not in the short time you've been here, and not down those steps." I walk towards him, raising my hand to trace the disc with my fingertips. Somehow it's covered with tiny etched lines I can feel but can't see, ordered to mean something to someone. "So what's going on?"

He takes a breath then huffs it out. "Look, if I were you, I'd turn around, go back up those steps and forget what you've seen here. Get whatever job that interview's for this afternoon…"

"So you have been listening."

"…or don't and stay and marry Detane…"

I glare at him. "Is that supposed to be a combination of Deacon and Tane?"

"Whatever, I don't care – just…"

"You know I have no interest in either of them." I move my hands to my hips. "Tane came to see me every weekend after my granddad died, all the way from the lighthouse – on the other side of the island. I dated him out of guilt. And Deacon, he's great on a bike but that's it. I've spoken to you way more than either of them."

"There's Sol."

I snort. "You think I could be with someone who sits at the end of the bar and stares at me?"

"Joey," he lowers his screwdriver, "I want…"

"No, let me tell you what I want. I want someone who shares my interests and passions, knows how they want the world to be and what they have to do to get it that way. Silly me, I thought that might be you, but I was wrong, my fault. I want a best friend who excites me. I also want someone who respects me enough not to humiliate me in front of everyone. Embarrassment doesn't look good on me."

"I… Joey, I'm sorry." His apology waits between us for an acknowledgment I'm not prepared to give. "Please understand, I like you…"

"Got a funny way of showing it."

"…but I come from a place where it would be really, really hard for you and I to be together. I don't want that for you."

"I'm perfectly able to decide what is and what isn't hard for me, thank you. Besides, we're not there, we're here." Until I leave tonight.

He focuses on the metal casing and frowns in thought.

"What would make it hard?" I have to ask. We haven't talked about faith. Does he subscribe to some extremist religion? Does he come from old money that would never welcome a girl from the islands? Is he a vegan? No. I shake my head. I would've picked up on something significant enough to make us incompatible. "I'm Australian," I shrug, "you're Australian – what's the problem?"

"I'm not Australian, Joey," he mutters, "that's the problem. I'm what you call an... immigrant."

"So? We need more immigrants. Anyone who complains about them only sees increased competition for jobs they want; they don't see that more people means more work and therefore more jobs. Every society needs fresh input, skills and drive, especially ours." I gesture towards Amama. "Maybe that's what the government should do, encourage immigrants to settle further out than the cities? Officer Hartono's an immigrant."

"I know. But that's not what I meant. Probably the wrong word."

"So what's the right word?"

"Alien?" He cringes.

I chuckle at his joke. Immigrant – alien – same thing. "Funny."

He looks up. "No, Joey. I'm serious. Look around. How *did* all this get in here? Even if those rocks weren't there, the stabiliser's much bigger than the hole they'd leave behind." He points at the disc. "This isn't Earth technology."

"What are you talking about?" I smile, looking from the disc to the rockfall and back. "It's high tech, that's for sure, but it's not 'alien'." Is it?

"Yes it is, Joey, and so am I."

"Don't be silly," I mutter, though can't take my eyes off the disc now. On its raised section, swirls coil and whorl in exact sequence with flows they would connect with were the section closed, though that's not possible. "Who've you been working with – army, ASIS, CIA, MI6, Intel?"

He shakes his head. "I come from a planet in the Gerund System. I'm not a ranger, Joey. I'm into environmental protection like you, except on a bigger scale: planetary climates. Earth is my current assignment."

I stare at him, gel dripping from his hands. No, not dripping. The gel hovers around his skin, not touching it, yet still moving when he moves.

"I'm sorry, I know it's a lot to take in. I'm not supposed to tell anyone. Obvious reasons."

"Yeah, right." I stammer. "You look human."

He glances at his body. "We haven't figured out yet if we came from Earth originally, or if you came from us. But, yes, we're similar enough for origins not to matter physically. Truth is, interplanetary relationships can be difficult on so many levels – someone always has to give up their home – but, maybe," a smile touches his lips as he looks me up and down, "now that you're here, maybe you're right and I shouldn't let that stop us from at least exploring what is between us. Couples have 'mated' before." He gives me a wink. "Fallen in love."

"Who said anything about love?"

He waits until I look into his eyes. "I'm saying it."

My breathing catches. The fire in his eyes is back.

"I've been holding back, Joey, trying to push you away." He steps closer. "Yet I find myself looking for you every day, hoping to see you, talk with you, be near you. And now you're here," his shoulders relax like he's giving up again, "and you've seen everything, I've no reason to hold back anymore. Do you want me to hold back?"

"No, um," I stammer again, reaching for the disc to steady myself. I miss the shell and my hand slips inside the raised section, touching the gel. It feels warm but cold, like a hundred miniscule lizards licking but not touching my skin. It feels… alien. It looks alien. "What?"

Matius drops his screwdriver, wipes his hands on his clothes and comes to my side, slides a hand around my waist to offer support. His thumb caresses the small of my back in comfort. "You understand why I couldn't tell you, until you found your way in here?"

I nod, speechless. We're finally touching.

"How did you find your way in here?" He asks in a whisper. "Were you following me?"

"Not exactly." I mumble, staring into his eyes. Of all the questions rushing around my mind, only one swirls to the top. "So, you do like me?"

He leans closer. "I do."

I smile, then take his face in my hands and kiss his lips like I want to live in them.

He enfolds me in his arms and moves his lips against mine with a hunger I knew was there as soon as we met. His intensity satisfies my own and brings me balance – he likes me, I knew it.

Our kiss slows into a lingering caress, then we break away and beam at each other.

"Now I need you to leave." He's serious. "Hartono's team, from the mainland, they'll be here any minute and their machines will detect my alien 'anomalies' more or less instantly, unless I can get this thing back up and running. I need at least half an hour."

"Why?" I ask, not taking my eyes off him. "What is 'this thing'?"

"A CAO Stabiliser. Been here forever, since the days of Lemuria and Atlantis – keeps things balanced." He gazes up at the disc. "Been breaking down for a few decades now though. It should have emitted its refurbishment signal to the manufacturers long before any compromise in its concealment shield, but things don't always go to plan. Sorry for all the mess."

I survey the cave floor, slowly, so I can accept what's right in front of me. "A few scattered tools is hardly a mess."

"I meant your global warming, climate change." He taps the stabiliser. "If it weren't for what's left of this, you'd be living in a furnace by now. And if I don't get it fixed…"

I stand on tiptoe to look inside the raised section, at the cylinders beneath it. The gel sinks down inside them. "They're tubes?"

"Yep," Matius says with pride, "each burrows deep into Earth's crust, far enough that together it can control tectonic plate motion, volcanism, thermohaline circulation and Earth's radiation budget."

"You mean, how the sun's energy gets distributed by ocean currents?"

He looks impressed.

"I do have an environmental degree, you know."

"Well, yes, it stabilises the albedo of continents, atmosphere and oceans, hence C-A-O Stabiliser. Without it, you're toast. And if I don't get these new parts installed in the next," he checks his watch, "twenty-five minutes, Hartono's team will detect anomalies behind that rockfall, then destroy everything when they blast it open. If I can get the concealment shield functioning again, though, they won't detect, see or hear anything, and I can carry on fixing the broken thermostatic components. Should take another month or so, quicker if I had another environmental scientist helping." He raises his eyebrows at me. "This could be it, Joey, the way you really save the world – all you have to do is keep my secret."

His body's warmth radiates into mine. "I can do that." I could.

"We'll only have a chance of course if I can conceal this thing in the next twenty-five minutes."

"How do you know they'll be here that soon?"

He points to a small portable screen beside the metal casing he was fixing. "Satellite imagery. There have already been some others poking around this morning, but this group is the one to worry about."

Reluctantly, I untangle myself from his embrace and move to see what he means. The screen is thin, bendy, with holographic 3D pixels that shift and move. I've never seen anything like it... on Earth. It shows the Cove Road, Quarry Road, the quarry itself and two helicopters zooming towards the island. They're probably closer to twenty minutes away. But it's okay because it all makes sense now – the reason Matius has been pushing me away, why I broke my shoulder and got rejected from the army – I'm on this island still because I need to be here today, to help Matius and save the world. "Fix what you need to fix. Leave the rest to me."

He picks up his screwdriver. "And you won't say anything?"

"I'll do better than that – I'll delay them for you, if you give me something in return."

His expression lifts. "Yes. Anything. Please."

I swim in his eyes as I step confidently towards him and kiss him again.

Again he drops his screwdriver.

This time our kiss is more of a confirmation. Yes to long chats about species preservation at sunset on the beach. Yes to not being able to keep my eyes off him. No to holding back. Yes, we're going to do this, regardless of what challenges it brings, including enabling Matius to finish his work, right here, right now.

"I should go," I say, breaking away and moving towards the passageway. When I reach it he's standing still, staring at me. "Hurry up," I tell him, "twenty minutes."

It spurs him into action.

I linger out of sight until I hear him sit back down and pull his metal casing towards him, scraping it across the floor. Ahead of me steps reach dimly into the rock, up and up. It took ten to fifteen minutes to climb down. It will take close to twenty minutes to climb up.

Not enough time.

I run forward and bound up the steps, my shadow wavering in front of the cave's ghostly white lighting. I scale step after step until my heart's pounding and I'm more out of breath than when pumping up Quarry Road, my chest heaving so much I have to slow to a scramble. I stagger on until my panting's more under control, then take a breath, swallow and burst into a run again. Time slips away. I'm barely going to make it.

The light behind me fades until I'm climbing in relative darkness. I trip, reach for the handrail groove, miss and thud onto my knees. My stomach flips at the thought of falling backwards. I steady myself, find the groove, then clamber up until, slowly, daylight gleams ahead. It brings some shape to the steps and I speed up again.

Soon the steps level into a path and my legs don't know what to do with the flatness, so tremble as I force them forward. When I emerge onto the ledge, I press my back to the rockface, squint against the light and ease them sideways, again and again. I have to reach my bike. I have to intercept Hartono's team and delay them somehow. I haven't even had time to think how.

I pause to take a breath and blink so my eyes can readjust to the light. I'll be quicker if I can see where I'm going.

"No, Joey!" someone yells. It's Hartono on the quarry floor beyond the water, her voice echoing across the lake. Her bob of peppered black hair shifts in the wind. A thick silver ring cuffs one ear. With her is a group of men and women – some in military uniform, others in t-shirts and shorts, all of them carry equipment on their backs. Behind them a helicopter's blades slow to a stop. "Wait," she yells, "you don't have to do this!"

They already know? I don't even know what I'm about to do.

"Yes," she continues, "you've been going through a tough time, so many important decisions to make. It must be hard without your mother to advise you. But we can help."

What is she talking about?

She steps towards the weedy water's edge. "You don't have to leave the island to pursue your career, Joey. My father was a scientist just like you, and he lived here consulting and writing reports. Your mother would be proud of you no matter what you do."

"You never knew my mother!" I shout down. I don't know why we're having this conversation but Hartono's whole team has stopped in their tracks. Exactly what I need. So wherever this is going, I'll go. "And you don't know anything about me!"

A military woman whispers something in Hartono's ear and takes off her backpack of equipment. She looks about my age. That could have been me.

"Don't come any closer," I warn her, "or I'll jump." It's what they think. And, to be honest, it could work. Island life thrives off restraint. But restraint might be the opposite of what I need right now. The lake's easily deep enough to break my fall. All I need is to distract them for a few minutes, pretend to be in trouble, force them to help me, delay things. Activists are known for being hot-headed. "I'll do it!"

Hartono whispers to the woman then turns back to me. "No one wants that, Joey, especially me. Alice would never forgive me. She cares so much for you. We all do. Please, come down and talk. We'll figure this out together. Why don't I call your dad? He'll come get you and we'll all have a nice cold beer, some roasted pig. It'll be so nice. I know how overwhelming choices like this can be; how hard it can be as an outsider adjusting to life in a small place like this. But outsiders bring life to the community – maybe you don't see it, how much everyone loves having you around, hearing about your ambitions and dreams. They follow your every move like it's their own because it is – you're our family. We're all here to support you, no matter what you choose, and there are so many options to take."

"I can only see one!" I yell, glancing down to check for submerged quarry stones. I'm a reluctant but strong swimmer; people say this lake's a bit cold for social swimming but the water below me is clear. I can see where the slabs of rock near Hartono graduate into the deep, and there's no such graduation near me; I can do this. This will be the perfect distraction.

"Please, Joey," Hartono shouts back. "I've never lost a soul on this island, don't be my first. I'm going to walk around the track now and help you up, okay?" She gestures at the track. "We can leave this lot to do what they've come to do and we can have that beer, or a cup of tea. The noise probably hasn't helped – you're tired from lack of peace and quiet, shaken from that continual racket. You can't make decisions under such stress, no one could. I'm coming up, okay?" She steps sideways.

"No!" I shout, straightening so I jump right. "I'm sorry, OHar, I truly am – but everyone's got to have a first." Then I lift a foot out over the hollow and leap forwards.

Hands clasped to my sides, I plummet through the air to the sound of Hartono screaming 'no' after me. All I can think is 'yes'. Matius needed half an hour. It took me twenty minutes to climb the steps. It will take Hartono's team at least five minutes to rescue me, another fifteen to ensure I'm okay before moving me back to Amama. This will give him plenty of time.

I hit the water firm and straight, shooting deep like an arrow fired at close range. It's freezing, much colder than I expected, and it stabs at me as I crane my neck back to look for the surface, more as I lift my arms to swim for it.

No, I can't. My bad shoulder twangs with pain and I flinch, bubbles escape. I level my arms and grip to cradle the nip of pain. I'll have to kick my way up and stroke one-handed.

I punt out my legs, though they spasm and tighten with cramp. I brace a foot against the opposite leg's shin, trying to release the contractions, but can't push hard enough before my foot slides off. I kick and push but the pain only intensifies. I glance up. The surface sparkles between blurred ripples of blue sky and grey rock. My chest burns and convulses. Why is this happening, I'm supposed to be up there by now. I don't want to breathe in any water. Maybe I'll simply float up?

No. My clothes and shoes are sodden and heavy and weigh me down. I don't float anywhere. I squirm against the cramp, more bubbles escape and, if anything, I sink. This isn't working.

I can't move my arms like I need.

I can't use my legs.

I'm running out of breath.

This was a mistake. I was supposed to save the planet – I can't even save myself.

I look up at the surface again and try wriggling towards it like a tadpole, convulsing like the muscles in my legs. The movement makes my head dizzy but I keep going. I need air. My lungs sting like I've inhaled boiling water. I can't give up.

The more I move, though, the more the dizziness in my head wobbles close to a faint. My eyes close by themselves and then everything's black and cold and wet. My head's so light it feels like floating. I wish I were, but I'm not. What have I done? Dad can't lose both wife and daughter. I needed to distract Hartono's team, that's all. Now I'm going to die in the cold and wet. I wanted to save the planet but not like this, not with my life.

Wait, yes I did.

The boom is so loud it jumps me out of my sleep and has my heart fluttering. I open my eyes to the ceiling beams of my bedroom, so white in the sunlight they're glary. I blink and refocus on the large floral figure bustling about my bed, picking up a dropped plate and biscuits.

"Alice?" I croak.

She swishes around as suddenly as Officer Hartono jumps up from a nearby chair. "Joey?" she murmurs. "You're awake." She beams her generous islander smile at me. "Now don't you worry about a thing, my girl. Dad's on his way back on the boat and we're going to work everything out."

"How am I here?"

"You don't remember?" Alice glances at OHar. "After they pulled you from the water, OHar had the helicopter bring you straight to me."

"I'll go wait by the harbour for your dad," OHar tells us both. "I'll fill him in, then had better get back. They're waiting for me."

Alice nods and reaches for OHar's shoulder. "Thank you."

OHar smiles back, then leans in to kiss Alice on the lips. "I'll see you at home tonight." She strokes Alice's plump cheek then strides out the door.

I thought Alice a spinster, unlucky in love. It didn't even occur to me that she and OHar were a couple.

Too wrapped up in my own life.

I open my mouth to say something but am too ashamed to speak.

"Hungry?" Alice asks once OHar's gone. She holds out her plate of biscuits.

I ease myself up in bed, then find my voice. "Have they found anything at the quarry yet, other than me?"

"Not yet. Still setting up their equipment."

I sigh in relief.

"You know, Joey," she sits on the chair, "I'm here if you want to talk about... things."

I shake my head. "I'm sorry, Alice, I can't." I have a secret to protect.

"But..."

"Please Alice, I'm really not up to it."

"Okay, Joey, I'm sure you've got good reason." It's what she said of Matius last night, a lifetime ago now.

"People usually do," I tell her, smiling and reaching for a biscuit.

"As your doctor I must recommend, however, that you reschedule your interview this afternoon. I need you to stay in bed and rest, your body's had a big shock."

"That's okay," I tell her, munching into a butter biscuit, "I won't be needing that interview now. I'm staying Alice, I'm staying on the island."

"Oh Joey," she leaps up to hug me. She feels warm and soft and snuggly. "That's wonderful news. And the right decision if you ask me. We'll find some way you can save the world from here."

"I have an idea already."

"Good, good," she says, sitting down again. "You might even be able to assist the specialists tomorrow, if you get a good night's sleep tonight."

"Something tells me I will."

"Do you think the noise will be something they can fix quickly?" she wonders, gazing out the window. "Looks like there might be a storm later."

"Who knows?" I tell her between bites. "It might not be something *they* can fix at all. It might even fix itself. But yes, it will be good not to jump out of my skin every night."

"Is that when you hear it, the noise?" Alice frowns.

"Wakes me up like clockwork: a boom, then a whistle, then a screech."

Alice shrugs. "Funny, I hear it differently."

"I guess we're all different. Different people can see and hear the same things in different ways."

Alice smiles and nods her head as she stands. "Even on a small island. Now get some rest."

I close my eyes, trusting Matius enough to know that I will. "Thanks, Alice."

Zena Shapter is the author of 'Towards White' (IFWG, 2017; the main character of which is Becky Dales) and the winner of over a dozen national writing competitions, including a Ditmar Award and the Australian Horror Writers' Association Award for Short Fiction. Her work has appeared in the Hugo-nominated 'Sci Phi Journal', 'Midnight Echo' (as well as their 'best of' anthology), 'Antipodean SF' and Award-Winning Australian Writing (twice). Reviewer for Tangent Online Lillian Csernica has referred to her as a writer who "deserves your attention". Her co-authored novel

'Into Tordon' (MidnightSun 2016) was distributed by Scholastic under the pseudonym Z.F. Kingbolt. She is the founder and leader of the Northern Beaches Writers' Group, a book creator and mentor, creative writing tutor, movie buff, traveller, wine lover and all round story nerd. Connect with her via zenashapter.com

We came to care as much as needed...

One Last Adventure

Emily Antonio

"Quail, and Durst," droned the Captain. I groaned at the scorching rays that shone through the trapdoor. "You're to go ashore and collect our season's supplies," he ordered in his gruff voice.

I was three-quarters asleep, having had limited rest after navigating at dawn. It was a miracle I was able to reply with the optimal, "Yes, sir."

The Captain took one look at my mate on the bunk below, drool mid-drop, and heaved a sigh. "And make sure Durst ain't going to bring any trouble. I don't want to have to find another dealer near these godforsaken islands. There's bad rocks so you'll be taking the single tinny. Remember to ask for Angel. Be back before dark." He glared at us, challenging our compliance, and spat on the floorboards in warning before stomping out the trapdoor.

The exiting thump of his boots woke Jim abruptly. "Yes sir!" He shot up, before falling off the bunk to the floor.

It was going to be an arduous trip.

The ship neared the island a few minutes later. It slowly greeted us from the horizon, a blurred mass, until we could make out a surprisingly rocky terrain. Great for hiking, if only we had the time.

Perhaps we would? I could do with stretching my land legs for a while. Jim had said the same only a couple of days ago. We'd talked about finding ourselves a bit of an adventure before taking leave in another month or so. Perhaps this island could deliver?

After readying the single, Jim and I disembarked the ship, and rowed in to the only docking cove. The customs station waylaid us, the elderly volunteer struggling to gather obscene amounts of information on our sailing passage, muttering this was the worst possible day we could have chosen. By the time we were free and officially on the land, we had rumbling bellies and sweaty brows from the heat.

"I vote we head to the pub," Jim grinned, only his mouth visible under his red flat cap that he wore wherever he went – it was garish and bright but a gift from his nephew. His nose was buried in the rudimentary map the customs lady had given us in pity of our haggard appearance.

"I don't think there is a pub, just a community centre. We should collect the supplies first, and pack them in before *any* kind of exploration, Jim," I pressed.

"But according to the trail, it's only about five hundred metres up that road! It is closer to the dock than the store, and this 'Angel' is more likely to be there than anywhere else. You can't knock that logic." His lip pouted. "Just a quick drink?"

I sighed. He was right. And it was turning out to be a humid day, so I was glad for the relief when we walked into the centre. The centre was a rough sight, its bricks cracked by weather and neglect, boards covered in peeling green paint. Over its front door was an old wooden sign, 'The Crusty'. Working at sea meant Jim and I had low expectations for any communal building in coastal towns, and this was no exception. 'The Crusty' was very accurate in name, though the insides were pleasantly welcoming – a sea of tables and chairs, and wooden floorboards leading onto a bright and breezy deck overlooking the harbour. The only occupants were one man behind the bar with a great brown beard that could have blanketed two children, and two men huddled over a corner table muttering animatedly to each other, one old and one young. The bartender was carving a roast pig big enough to feed fifty people.

"I don't suppose there's any chance of finding women around, eh?" Jim whispered to me, eyeing the bearded man behind the bar. "One pint of..."

I elbowed Jim in the ribs.

"Where can we find an Angel?"

The bearded bartender stared at us blankly, giving no recognition he had heard me. I moved my weight uneasily to my other foot, interrupted by my wince as an elbow caught me in the gut in retribution.

"Do you happen to know an Angel?" I tried again, straightening my stance.

"Are you trying to be funny?" The bartender narrowed his eyes at us. "Is this what I've got to look forward to with you lot today?" He grimaced and pointed his carving knife at us both in turn. "I understand the need to let off steam under pressure, but tell your superiors they won't get nothing from us with lip like that. We're here to help, not amuse, so how about you buy something or get out?"

"Fine by me!" Jim cheered. "Two of, uh, this one please," he pointed to the unfamiliar tap.

The bartender worked silently.

When the glasses landed on the bar – one touching down a markedly shorter time than the other – and coins were exchanged, I looked to the intimidating man expectedly. "We still need to find an Angel. Captain Krishner sent us."

He heaved a weary sigh, arms resting heavily on the bar. "Why didn't you say so before, aye? Come round 'ere," he beckoned behind the bar.

We followed him towards the sound of two women talking in a backroom, though he diverted into a small storage space. And there it was, a neat little pile of crates of supplies that the Captain had requested.

Jim moved his hand to flip the lid of a crate, curious.

I slapped him away, only to receive a punch in the gut.

"So, you're 'Angel'?" Jim queried, eyebrows raised.

I leant on the wall for support, winded.

"Family name," he curtly supplied, eager to end the interaction. "Door's unlocked 'til sundown," he gestured at the pile. "Pick it up whenever you feel. You must be, er," he mumbled, watching Jim down the rest of his pint in quick fashion, "glad to be on land for a few hours." He led us back to the bar.

"We are," I finished my beer too.

"Best beer I've had in months, mate!" Jim said as we continued on towards the front door. "What's your source?"

"We make it locally," was all Angel said.

Then we were back out in the sun, free to explore the island without the Captain, with hours until dark. We looked to each other, grins spreading as the idea of freedom bloomed. I was about to query what we should do, having not been on land for seven months, when the two men huddled at the table from the centre burst through its door and nearly took us to the ground.

With no apologies, the younger man continued on, struggling to lift the weight of the older man – trying to find an arm, a shoulder, to provide support to his drunken walk.

"No more," the older one moaned, dressed in a grubby overcoat despite the heat pressing down on the island. "Don't take me back there."

"I'm not!" the taller, younger man pleaded.

"Excuse me," Jim interrupted. "Where's a good place to start exploring this island?"

"No, no," the older man moaned, staring at where the road cornered around a limestone boulder covered in ferns. "Not the water."

"Shh, pops," the younger one whispered. He eyed us, and I shrank back from his hostility. "It's not a good day for a visit… we're

about to be flooded with a group of specialists from the mainland."
He started to pull the other man forward, before turning back to
us. "Though there'd be no harm in the campgrounds, I suppose,
mainlanders usually check that out, and there's a pretty jungle
beach not far from here – they should be quiet and out of the way
enough."

"Out of the way of what?"

"Everyone. Best keep out of everyone's way today," he warned.

"No," his father moaned, thrashing around, this time addressing
us. "Don't pass by over there, you'd have to go past the water, the
awful water…"

The younger man whispered a few calming words to his father.
"Just stick to the main trails on your map there," he then ordered
us, "and nowhere else."

I watched the two of them hobble off down the road, my
brow scrunching at their oddity. "Well, that was an unexpected
welcome..." I started to say to Jim, only he wasn't by my side.

"C'mon," he yelled, gesturing for me to follow. "Can't you hear
it? Adventure awaits!" He was already on the other side of the road
and disappearing around the limestone boulder.

I rounded the corner to find him pulling bush apart like there
was no tomorrow, trudging through the straggly branches and
wiry trees. "Jim, they already don't like newcomers, don't smash
their land about! According to the map, the road continues up and
around to the campgrounds without the need for..." I was puffed
by the time I was at his side, realising what he was so adamantly
reaching towards. "Oh."

"Do you think that's the water the mad fellow was whining
about?" Jim asked, pointing through the gap he had cleared to a
sign reading: 'Quarry Lake: 4km'. Beyond it was a narrow track,
encumbered by nature. "Looks like a shortcut to me." He wiped
sweat from under his flat cap.

"If it is, then we definitely shouldn't go that way. It's not on the map."

"Darren, we've had many adventures at sea, let's at least explore the possibility of one on land. You wanted to have one last adventure before taking leave in the winter, didn't you? A send off? We talked about this. Let's take the road less travelled by, come on! Who wants to go to another boring beach? Not me!"

I sighed and peered at the sign again, the narrow track, previously hidden by overgrown bush. It did peek my interest: going somewhere we weren't supposed to go, where few people did now, it seemed. Jim and I had been at sea on and off for a decade, but when the warm weather died I didn't just plan to take winter leave – I planned to move on. I needed to get back to land permanently. The sea does things to your head.

"Okay. We'll check it out."

Jimmy's euphoric response resulted in bodily harm – another punch in my guts.

I rubbed at my side and followed his jog down the track, my lips curling up. One last adventure.

The track was tight scrub and had crisp bush stems at just the right height to catch you bloody on your side. After what felt more like twenty kilometres of hacking, the bush descended down towards a crossroads with another, larger well-used track, resembling a road in places, then opened onto a small glass lake backed by tall curving cliffs, scored like quarry walls. I looked at my map. There was an old quarry marked on the island, and this one looked disused for decades. Bush circled the smooth, silent water of the lake and crept over an old vehicle track leading up the cliff's south side towards its rim.

"Oi, mate. Get over here." Jim was like a fox to a rabbit hole. He was at the base of the vehicle track, leaning as if straining to hear something. "Do you hear that?!" he asked, panic wavering in his voice. "Christ, I think someone's hurt!"

A terrifying noise came swimming down the track, rushing at our faces – a loud boom followed by painful groans.

"We've got to get up there!" I shouted, not allowing shock to settle in. Someone needed our help.

I was faster than Jim because of his liquid belly and scaled the track so rapidly I only glanced at the signage in the sloping bush at its base, which was spray-painted with Xs, skulls and bones. It was an odd type of vandalism, but I dismissed it to delinquent kids, and it barely caused my step to hesitate.

Soon I was at the crest, skidding on loose rocks when I tried to slow to gather my bearings. The sky was bright, and even though I wasn't physically high enough, the air felt thinner. Blood pumped fast and my hearing was overwhelmed, sensitive to the bird whistles and snapping of twigs in among the bush.

The groans and booming claps grew louder, snapping me out of my trance. My eyes searched the crest wildly, frantically searching, expecting a person with grievous injury, but coming up empty. Where were they?

A few further steps forward and I stared down a sheer drop of rock which landed straight in a shining stillness of deep water. It was a stunning view, made horrific by the gut-wrenching wails sounding around and echoing in the still space.

"Where are you?" I called desperately into the quarry, though my own voice failed to echo and travel.

"D-Darren?" Jim puffed when he reached my side, dropping to the ground on his hands and knees in exhaustion. "Where are they?" he wheezed out.

"There's nothing here." It was the only answer I could provide.

"What do you mean?" He queried, once able to stand up straight again. "The noise was coming directly from here. It was..." he spun around, though the quarry was suddenly silent, "...it was, from the water?" He trailed off weakly.

It was an unlikely answer as the water was smooth as could be.

Standing on the edge of the cliff, peering down, my stomach tied itself in knots. The smoothness of the water and loudness of the noise was nagging at the back of my mind. If it weren't for my curiosity and dread about following the terrifying noise, my gut instinct told me to leave right then.

But Jim made my decision for me when he sped back down the slope that lead to the base of the quarry, no regards for the debris of branches he left in his wake. His bright red flat cap bounced away from me, and he was out of my sight within seconds. I followed his trail, careful not to slide down the jagged rock edge.

About halfway down and the base of the quarry in my sights, I heard the booming noise again, louder and deeper than it had been at the crest. Directly after, there was a yell from Jim. The groans and claps of thunderous sound reverberated around the quarry. The water shifted down below; ripples and waves sloshed at the rock. Movement, finally.

My breath quickened when I heard no other noise from Jim. "Jim! Jim, do you hear that? Do you see anyone?" I was breathless and concentrating on the rest of my descent; I couldn't get any easy footholds.

I rounded the base of the quarry and ran onto a beach of pebbles and rocks of varying shades of grey, all blended together. I swivelled, skidding in loose rocks, expecting to find Jim and the source of the noise. But there were only weeds. Weeds that were up to my chest.

"Jim!" I called. My voice echoed throughout the quarry, bouncing back from the impenetrable rock: Jim, Jim, Jim… It circled around to haunt me. "Jim!" I cried with more urgency. "This isn't funny," I added, in case he was pranking me.

The noise boomed and my head reflexively flicked to the right, where the water met the pebbles in small waves. I ran, trusting my hearing, and ignored the burning of my calves. My gut clenched and turned, not liking the claustrophobic quarry. I ripped apart the bush, but could see no movement ahead.

"Jim!" My voice became hoarse and frantic. I couldn't see anything in the water. I was contemplating jumping in when the noise stopped.

An eerie stillness hung in the air; even the birds were silent.

Freaking me out, I scanned the quarry and the crossroads behind me, noticing an arrow sign saying: 'Campsite: 3km'. All rational thought was gone, I just needed to get to some people. Other people would know what to do.

I ran for what felt like an hour before I saw anything resembling civilisation. The dirt and limestone path led to the basic foundations of a camping ground: a well, outhouse, and brick kitchen. A middle-aged woman was by the well, bucket swinging and hand shielding her eyes from the sun. I hadn't realised the sun was beating down on me until that moment, but there was no time for thoughts of heat stroke.

"Mam!" I spluttered out of my dry throat. "Please, Mam. My friend…" I leaned down, my hands on my knees as I struggled for breath. Dehydration tore at my throat.

The woman took pity on me and came over at a trot. "Dearie, are you alright? You're not from around here, best to take water when you wander off. Here, this is good enough to drink." She handed me her bucket and I gulped like an empty camel.

"My friend," I spluttered, "he's disappeared."

The woman's face flickered between concerned and serious. Her eyes darted around the open area in what was unmistakably fear.

I glanced around myself, for dangerous animals.

"Where was he at, when you lost sight of him?" she asked sharply.

"The base of the quarry."

"Oh, good lord," she swore. "We've got to get them in as soon as possible," she mumbled to herself. "Another one. This time there's no chance to argue."

She nibbled her lip, and squinted at me. I was still trying to catch my breath.

"Lucas!" she bellowed swiftly in the other direction.

A moment later a young boy, only up to her elbow, came running over.

"What, Ma?"

"Radio the station," she paused, scratching her chin. "Tell them that the mainlanders need to speed up today. There's been a missing fella. Collect them all and tell them I'm at the quarry with a," she gave me a once-over, "with a newcomer. What's your name?"

"Darren."

"I'm Marlene."

———

"This was where you were? When you lost 'im?" Marlene queried.

"Yes," I answered, standing around the base where I had seen the water move.

We'd been at the quarry for a half hour and the thunderous noise continued, but the echo made it impossible to decipher from which direction it originated. The sky was darkening with clouds on the horizon, which created another problem in distinguishing the noise from distant rumbles of thunder.

"Oh, thank the heavens," Marlene breathed a heavy sigh of relief.

A group of islanders were entering the base of the quarry, some carrying torches, rope and other equipment.

The reinforcement of people was comforting. They spread out to search for Jim immediately.

"Officer Hartono," said a Japanese woman in officer attire. She greeted me with a firm hand. "Now let's make this quick. I've already dealt with several emergencies this morning and the mainlanders are due any minute." She began firing questions at me about Jim's disappearance. "We'll do everything we can, Darren," she said after the interrogation, watching over the search party.

I snorted. About a dozen of the town's residents were searching the quarry from head to toe. Even Angel was helping, but it was nothing that I hadn't already done. "Is this your big strategic search?" I asked sarcastically.

"No, actually," she fiddled with her notepad, flipping it several times to make sure the papers were smooth. "The mainland team will instigate a full investigation. Or is that still not up to your standards, Quail?" she asked, eyebrow raised. "I'm sure they will prioritise your friend over even more pressing matters."

"Oh," I replied, taken aback. "What pressing matters?" My thoughts raced.

Hartono's gaze shifted from the volunteers to the water. She pursed her lips, reluctant to answer. "There have been… complaints already, around the safety of the quarry. Noises and such." She waved off with a hand and a forced laugh.

I stood still in disbelief. Before I could argue her minimisation, she was called over by the young man Jim and I'd met outside the pub.

The two of them whispered together, heads huddled, before Hartono's shoulders sagged.

I started to carve my way through the weeds to them when she turned around, lips pursed and eyes focused on an item in her hands. My eyes travelled down to see her holding Jim's bright red flat cap, wet and limp.

A strangled sound escaped my throat. Jim? "That's his."

My confirmation made the group's efforts double. The mysterious noise was still reverberating around the quarry every so often, each time inducing cringes and a renewed vigour in their work.

Soon after, however, the clouds grew darker drawing an oppressive shadow over the quarry, and there was a hum.

I twisted my head around, trying to pinpoint the hum that caused us to stop in our steps.

"Everyone," Hartono announced over a megaphone, "clear the quarry and gather on Quarry Road. The mainlanders are here."

The hum grew louder until it droned over our heads, revealing a large grey monster blanketing the sky as it crossed directly over the quarry. The helicopter circled around to land on the road itself. A team of five, ten, fifteen hopped out onto the impromptu dirt tarmac, and jogged in file over to Officer Hartono. One of the females in uniform had a brief conversation with Hartono, and then turned to the group at large.

"My name is Inspector Haze." Her voice was confident, demanding attention and obedience. "I will be directing this investigation and any surrounding disappearances."

"Disappearance-s?" I angrily grouched at Hartono. "Just how many disappearances have occurred?!"

"We had warned the locals of not approaching the quarry alone," she told me. "But we weren't aware any newcomers were here." Seeing Hartono's downtrodden gaze, and the local volunteers who gave Inspector Haze their entire attention, I realised some grave misfortune had fallen upon this island.

Inspector Haze quickly delegated search parties to quadrants. My party included Angel, Eliza – an adolescent who was fascinated by some alleged 'paranormal' properties of the quarry – and a slow elderly man named Douglas who really ought to have stayed home. We set off into the bush.

Behind us at the quarry I heard Hartono shouting at someone, a girl shouting back, a splash, then the helicopter took off somewhere, or another helicopter landed. Either way, we weren't called back so we kept searching. Whatever else was going on today, Jim was my priority.

"The quarry shut down two decades ago," Douglas told me as we searched in the grassy hollows on the south-west side of the base. "The noise first started for me when Eliza here's older sis gone missing."

My eyes jumped to the sour young adult with dark hair that fell into her eyes.

"She didn't go missing," Eliza burst out stubbornly. "She was taken by something. Everyone could hear the noises afterwards, and the loud clashes. She didn't run away like Mama said."

Eliza gave me a dark look, warning me before I could even think to disagree.

"Everyone loved that girl, they did," the old man, Douglas, conceded. "Kind as anything."

Eliza smiled. "She had the curliest brown hair you could imagine. Ringlets that would spring back after they were pulled. Always did her work, always home on time." Eliza suddenly turned her gaze to the ground, subdued. "Until one day she wasn't."

"Well she was havin' trouble..."

"Stephie wasn't having trouble with anything!" Eliza glared at Douglas. Her search through the grass became violent, thrashing leaves like she was drowning in them.

"What do you think they're going to find?" I murmured to Angel quietly, while the elderly Douglas bickered with a vehement Eliza.

Angel grunted. "Can't be human. Everyone's been watched around here the last few weeks so much that there's no privacy no more. It's lucky you even docked today, port's tightening up too until this is resolved. Now it looks like a storm's blowing in."

"Oh, shit." What if I couldn't get back to the ship? "Captain's going to go nuts if I don't get those supplies to him, even when he finds out Jim's gone missing. Probably blame it all on Jim, actually." I frowned to myself, glancing up at a sun now completely buried by clouds. Somewhere offshore, a storm was definitely brewing.

"Hey, I can sneak ya back to 'The Crusty' if you need to get it back to the ship. This lot," he gestured to the mainlander team, "they won't let you go if you ask for permission. Best we do it quietly, so you can get your shipment out and come back before they notice ya missing. They'll find Jim, don't worry. You can rejoin the search after? This way Krishner will understand, might even come help himself."

He might. "Thank you, Angel. Your help is a..."

"Aye, leave the frilliness now," he grumbled, twisting his hat in his hands. "You ain't the first one who lost a buddy because of this quarry. Not that he's lost…"

⸻

Angel and I snuck away under the cover of Eliza and Douglas upping their argument. We were at the community centre twenty minutes later, racing the looming cloud cover that now spat on us.

"I'll watch out here in case anyone wanders by," Angel barked over the whistling wind.

"You're actually a great mate, Angel." I gave his hand a rough shake, and swear I saw a half-grimace smile on his face.

The centre was dark inside, though I could hear women talking in the back again. I fumbled for the lights, then gave up and headed straight to the back store room. Its light was already on, I could see it seeping under the doorframe. I slowed my steps, heart rate rising; nobody was supposed to be here. I just wanted to grab the bags and hightail it to the cove before any storm hit and I was stuck here. I pushed the door open to the room cautiously, before jumping at the inhabitants.

"Jim!" I yelled in shock.

My mate was slumped on the ground beside our small crates of supplies. There was an empty bottle of whiskey beside him and a woman's head of curls on his shoulder.

"Jim!"

My voice woke him up and his hand went straight to his temple. "Ouch, mate," he whined, closing his eyes against the light. "Be mindful of the weary, yeah?"

"Where the fuck have you been? The whole town's out there looking for you, and you're drinking by yourself?!"

The girl stirred.

"Not entirely by myself," he smirked.

I kicked him in the shin.

Jim whimpered. "Okay, okay, let's head back. He slid out from under the girl and rose to leave her still snoozing softly.

"Well, we've got to settle all this with the town first. They're worried sick."

"What's taking so long?" Angel stopped in the doorway. He looked from my mate, to the woman asleep, to the empty bottle of hooch Jim had obviously stolen. His face turned puce.

"You bloody faked it all, didn't ya! Get outta my property, you good for nothin' seaman! Out!" he screeched, fumbling behind the bar for a baseball bat.

"Jim, Jim, grab the goddamn supplies!" I yelled as Angel turned from ally to a man on a revenge mission.

We dived for the crates and escaped out the back door, running straight for the cove. The old customs lady must have been at the quarry, as we had a clear line to the single. We ploughed through the choppy water as fast as we could. The situation was so ridiculous that by the time we were past the breakwater we couldn't help but laugh in hysterics.

Jim's laughter broke first, then he started wheezing.

"Mate, you alright?" I asked, pumping a hand on his back to help cough the air out.

"Mm, mm yeah. One sec," he said, and twisted around to a crate, bringing out one fine bottle of whiskey and taking a gulp.

I gaped. "That's what we were collecting for the Captain? I was put through the wringer for some bloody bottles of whiskey?"

"What wringer, mate?" Jim asked in between sips.

"Fuck," he breathed in, "my ribs are a bit painful though." He pulled his shirt up to reveal a purple and blue side.

"Shit, Jim! That looks bad. What happened to you?"

"Well, I..." he faltered. "There was the quarry, then there was this woman, and Angel's bar had a stocked kitchen, so..." he laughed, trembling a bit when he traced his side. "Must've bashed myself somewhere along the way," he frowned in confusion, rubbing his temple. "And lost me flat cap."

The rain hit before we reached the ship, coating us to the bone. All I could do was chuckle at the misfortune of the day.

"Well, I'm glad you weren't eaten by a quarry monster," I laughed. "One last adventure, hey," I grinned. "Oh, and who was the woman you were with, anyway?"

"Picked her up at the quarry, actually. A real cutie. Her name was Stephie."

Emily Antonio is a writer and librarian who dabbles in writing fiction for children and young adults in her spare time. A background in psychology and love of horror films influence her writing in unique ways. She is currently working on a series of short stories.

Sometimes we care too much and too long...

No Matter How You Look At It

Suzi Green

One, two, three, four, five, six. I let out another silence-shredding scream. In my head I counted the breaks between the waves hitting the rocks below. I let rip again, making my throat sore. Five, six, again. Each scream offered relief, like a cutter slicing through their own skin. Again. That one caught in my throat and made me cough.

From where I stood on North East Point, I could see at least a mile across the ocean, lit by a large distant moon. I watched the next wave hit the base of the cliff. Directly above, the midnight stars were hidden by increasingly thickening clouds. I closed my eyes, and tried to imagine the waves rolling gently onto a beach where children might play. The children would be laughing. Then they'd be laughing at me. Suddenly I screeched again, this time without the colliding water to dull the sound. The piercing noise made me cup my hands over my ears. I heard my heart beating. So fast.

"Where the fuck have you been Min? Its 1am," Roj asked as I crawled into bed next to him. I considered telling him the truth, that I'd been up at The Point, looking down, wondering whether or not to jump. "Just round the other end of the cove." I saw no merit in honesty.

Roj turned over to face me in the dark. I wondered if my husband knew I was lying. If he'd really wanted to know where I was, he could've tracked my phone. Perhaps he already had. He gave me that final kiss, the one he always did before he rolled over to sleep.

I listened. Within seconds his breathing slowed. He was so calm. I felt my shameful resentment for the ease with which he'd adapted to island life. Nothing seemed to bother him.

Not wanting to be the only one awake, I childishly kicked my feet into the mattress, and complained, as I did every night, about the incessant noise.

Roj woke, rolled back to stroke my face. "You can hardly even hear it tonight."

"It's driving me mad, especially the not knowing." I put my hands over my ears again, mirroring my earlier actions, accidentally reminding me of my inner pain. "Not knowing is the worst. If I knew I might feel better."

He grabbed my wrists and pulled my hands away.

"Perhaps it's the sound of doom." I could tell from his tone of voice that he was smirking. "You once said this island is close to hell." That had been a dark day. Roj mimicked the mesmeric booming sound with his low bass tones, making himself laugh. "Maybe it's your biological clock ticking really deeply."

I faked a laugh and slapped him on the arm. I wanted him to think that I saw the funny side so I didn't have to explain how I really felt. As the lights were out, I didn't bother to smile.

"Well, we could always..." Roj slid his hand onto my stomach, "it has been a while since we... and surely that is our purpose on this island." He made a heart shape with his fingers around my belly button.

I wriggled, and moved his hand back to his side of the bed. "Don't say that."

Roj ran through the same argument he always did. There were engineers, a teacher, a nurse... What skills did we have? I hadn't even bothered to tell people on the island about my PhD. What good was a doctorate in Advanced Mathematics for being a shopkeeper in the middle of the ocean? At the time, I'd been desperate to leave my consumerist, twitter-addicted, money-driven life to live in a peaceful loving community. It wasn't what my Post-Doc supervisor had envisaged for me. And apparently now our sole purpose here was procreation.

But tonight the noise really was driving me completely mad. I couldn't cope, especially when Roj just wanted to go on as if everything was okay – and have a baby. How could we bring a baby into this insanity?

"Well," Roj sounded resigned, "if I'm not getting any sex, I'm going to get some sleep. We have to open up in five hours."

I grabbed my tablet off the bedside table and clicked through to where I'd saved my daily list of instructions. I was pretty sure we'd been told to stay indoors while the investigation was underway.

"Oh screw the rules. I think that's why you wanted to come here. You like it when someone takes charge." Roj made another move on me, trying to grab my wrist and hold it over my head in a mock-bondage move. But it went wrong, I lost control of the tablet and it landed, screen-side down, smack on the side of his face.

"Ha, okay, you win." He blurted, trying to pretend the 970g brick didn't hurt. He gave up and rolled away.

Still awake and staring into the semi-darkness, I found myself thinking about changing the shop layout. The children's toys and clothes were in the first aisle so that we could keep an eye on things from our podium position at the counter, which ran the whole length on one of the short sides. But the kids' food was right at the back of the third aisle. It seemed a bit cruel to have them diagonally opposite, but it made people walk around the whole store, which made them buy more things. At least we'd moved the confectionary to aisle two. When it was previously stacked in front of the till, Roj just couldn't help himself; now all that remained was the chewing gum.

I tried to empty my mind so I could sleep, like the relaxation podcast said. At first I was still at the shop counter, but then as I looked over it to the ground, it got further and further away.

Suddenly I was up on the cliff again. I tried to move away from it, above it, so I could trace the edge with my finger like I did when I looked at the big map of the island. I liked the fractal coastline, a never-ending shape which repeated itself no matter how you looked at it. Whether with a magnifying glass or from hundreds of miles away with a satellite image, the pattern infinitely repeated. Like the thoughts in my head.

Shit, I really needed to snap out of it.

The next morning, life was normal, and very quiet. I'd been working on the store layout, trying to maximise the 8m x 10m shelved area that attempted to contain all the essentials for every island resident. Aisle one was fridges and the fresh grocery. Aisle two was dry foods. Aisle three was cleaning, toiletries, baby things and stationery. On the back wall there were some upright freezers, and in every corner I'd been adding extra freestanding carousels, to hold everything from cards and costume jewellery to pliers and pepper pots.

By lunchtime, Roj and I were behind the main counter measuring up to see if we could make space for a proper espresso coffee machine. There was a ding, and the door swung open against the stopper designed to prevent it slamming against the first row of shelves.

"Oh thank God you're open, I need more formula." Fran Ritsun belted down the end aisle with her podgy six-month old baby on her hip. "I got a whole new tin yesterday, but it was a casualty of the jealous terrible-twos," she called, as she practically ran the twelve steps it took to get from one end of the shop to the other. As she bent down to pick up baby food, her older child broke loose from the runner-reigns recommended for island parenting. He ran around the shop, ending by crashing into the main counter, right in front of Roj and me.

Roj stretched over and pulled up the little squirmer to sit on the counter. "You're getting big aren't you." Roj turned him around so his back was to his approaching mother, and pulled a face that suggested the child could probably do with missing a meal. I giggled. Thank God for Roj, my Syrian ray of sunshine. With one hand still firmly on the child, he swiped the formula over the scanner so the price presented itself on the customer-facing screen.

"Fran?" he asked, though got a glare in response. "Sorry. Mrs Ritsun."

Her formality was so out of place with the rest of the island. "Mr Iyen?"

I could tell he wanted to say, call me Roj, but he resisted. "Do you know what they're doing in there today, at the quarry? Doesn't your partner do casual work for Hartono?"

"She does, but you know she can't tell me. And I couldn't say anything about it, even if she had told me. Which of course she hasn't." She held her son close to her, as if even hypothetical indiscretion might impact her family. "None of us know anything."

"Oh, I didn't mean anything by it. Sorry." He wiped his brow and despite the space between us, I could tell he was getting clammy. "Some of us just really need to know." He glanced at me.

"Good day Mr Iyen, Mrs Iyen." She nodded at me as she ushered her eldest out the door, the other still stuck to her hip.

As soon as Fran left the shop, we huddled behind the counter. Roj elbowed me in the side. "Did you see the look on her face? Why didn't you say something too?"

I smiled. "I thought I'd let you try a charm offensive." I knelt down to straighten the pile of last weeks' newspapers stacked under the counter.

"But she's gay," laughed Roj. I could see he was pleased that I still thought him charming. He nudged his knee into me, and I leant back onto his legs, practically sitting on his feet.

"It's not like lesbians are immune to charming men, it's just such a rare occurrence that they date women instead." I grinned up at him. It was the first time I'd relaxed in ages.

I twisted around and pulled his zipper down.

"Oh Min, we shouldn't really, not if…" But I'd already placed his cock in my mouth and was swirling it around with my tongue. "Oh shit Min. Oh my God. But what about baby-sex? And we might get caught."

I grabbed hold of his hips and crouched a little lower, so no matter how you looked at it, all you'd be able to see was Roj's upper body. I kept sucking. This way I had control over the purpose of his orgasms.

"Oh Min," Roj cried while he gripped the edge of the shop counter.

He smacked his hand on the island's Community Newsletter as he came.

"Can you keep an eye on things while I go for a run?" It was a rhetorical question. Roj had already changed into his shorts and t-shirt, the ones his father had brought him from Syria after he finally got out too.

I stood up and noticed Roj's eyes peering at the space in front of me. I shifted position so he no longer had a direct line of sight to the children's toys and clothes display.

"Are you actually going for a run, or are you just trying to get near the quarry, to find out what's going on?" For me?

"It's fine. I'm just going to run our normal route: round the point to the waterfall and then back over the top. I'm wearing the tracker," he tapped his wrist strap, "so you'll be able to see where I am at all times." He laughed. We both knew I would track him anyway.

"But Roj, sweetie." I didn't want him to go. We weren't supposed to go near the place. I wanted to know, of course, to see what he could find out about the noise, about the investigation. Not knowing was the worst. But what if he got caught? Fran had become protective of her children just talking about it, as if something might happen to them because of her. Surely, though, he wouldn't get into that much trouble for simply wanting to see the investigation team at work – it was a public space? I caressed his bare arm and gently squeezed his bicep. The promise of sex was normally enough to distract him, especially if I agreed to play Russian roulette without a condom, but I'd already played that hand this morning.

"Just a quick run, while the shop is quiet." The corners of his mouth turned up. It was never anything other than quiet in the shop. There hadn't been a rush here, ever. This late in the afternoon it wasn't likely to be either. He moved toward me. "And later, it would be a good time to try tonight, wouldn't it?" He reached over to the twirled sleeve of a cute baby onesie he'd added to the inventory a few months earlier.

I pulled it away from him and ushered him out the door.

I stared after him, long after his long running legs had disappeared.

I zipped round the counter to the main computer. I tapped in the password, and double clicked on the tracking app. I was hypnotised by the screen, watching Roj's dot trekking along the coastline. That barren coastline, the obstacle to our future. Roj was so desperate to become a father, but he only imagined the good times. I couldn't get past the thought of something going wrong. We were so isolated. Helicopters, even boats couldn't always land if the wind wasn't in the right direction. And the idea of having trouble in labour, or a sick baby, no matter how you looked at it – it just seemed too much of a risk.

So instead, I'd dreamt up this other idea; an absurd fucked-up fantasy. I'd never told Roj, or anyone for that matter. The fact that I even had the thought was good enough reason for me not to bear children. But in the world that I invented, in the darkest part of my subconscious, I imagined that in the middle of the island, where the noise had started coming from, there was a group of people trapped underground. I imagined that the constant noise was the sound of them trying to chisel their way out. And within that group of prisoners, there was an orphaned child, whose parents had been crushed in some disaster, and that we would be called upon to adopt, as we were the only married couple on the island without any children.

The screen continued to blip. My eyes went dry from staring. And suddenly there was someone staring right at me.

"Hello?"

"Oh, hello, Philo." I tried not to appear startled, but the look on her aged face suggested I had failed.

"Didn't mean to scare you!" Philo raised her eyebrows and I noticed a tweak at the side of her lips. I'd seen Philo, short for Philomena, almost every day since we'd moved to the island. She was the kind of person who shopped for company. I liked her. I could tell she'd been a rebel in her younger days. She was the one person who I might consider telling my shameful fantasy, though hadn't had the courage yet. I swiped her margarine and malt loaf and the price flashed up on the till.

"How come you're so comfortable, Philo, being you, and here on an island like this? You seem so calm, doesn't the noise drive you nuts?"

The old lady peered as if looking over half-moon glasses, even though there were none. "I don't think I know what you mean, dear. I can only be me. And I like being here. The island is so peaceful. What noises do you hear?"

For a moment I wondered if Philo might be somewhat deaf, or if the noise was in my head, along with my other fantasies. I had hoped my stress would disappear once my PhD was over – a doctorate in chaos theory, for the person with the chaotic mind, now that's irony. But perhaps it hadn't.

"Oh Minna," Philo continued, noticing my expression, "no

matter how you look at it, this is all you have now, it's all any of us have, so you gotta make the most of it. Don't let any of the other nonsense get to you – the quarry and all. You just focus on what you and your husband want. Or don't want."

Dazed, I went back to the computer after Philo left. 'And don't want.' What was she trying to tell me? And what did she know about the quarry?

One thing she was right about was that life *should* be about me and Roj. My Syrian sunshine. No matter how shit I felt, he was always there, brightening my life. I felt calm again, and smiled at the memory of our simple Kurdish-Christian wedding. I'd worn a classic white dress, was covered with Kurdish Henna body art and received the 'Shara Buke' shawl as a sign of my acceptance into the Kurdish family. Roj even sang a traditional Kurdish love song accompanied by his father playing the Tanbur. And his small group of family and friends managed to get the whole group holding hands to attempt a traditional Syrian dance.

Scanning the screen, I looked for the dot of Roj's tracker around the waterfall, where he said he'd gone for his run. I couldn't see him.

I zoomed out. He was way off route. His dot was at the entrance to the quarry.

Shit. I shouldn't have let him go. What was he doing there? Hell, I knew what he was doing there. He was letting the nonsense about the quarry get to him. Or maybe the nonsense that was getting to me. He was there to find out for me. Oh Roj. I stroked the blue dot on the screen. He had to be okay out there.

I pottered around the store. I couldn't concentrate, but he'd be back soon. Roj was a good runner. A lot faster than me, he strolled when we went running together, his long legs stretching one for every two of my steps. And he was wearing that outfit with what he called his 'go faster stripes'. I smiled at his silliness, I loved that he managed to find every little ounce of joy in life. For him, island life was blissful, compared to the warzone in which he'd been brought up – literally, an area in North Syria, full of other Kurds who had already fled from Iraq, and who eventually were forced to escape Syria too. Everything in his past was tinged with battle wounds, more psychological than physical. But that's what made him smile, and find the funny side of everything. And also, it was what made him think he was bloody invincible.

I went back to the computer, expecting to see him nearly back at the store. He'd be doing his hamstring stretches on the bench on the corner, or calf stretches against the old flag pole. But his dot was still in the same place, by the quarry.

"Roj, what are you doing?" Gripping the old PC monitor, I interrogated it for all it was worth. Never taking my eyes off the blue dot, I willed it to move. Another minute or two passed, maybe longer. He was still in the same place. My heart got louder and my throat drier. "Move, damn it. Move!"

Then there was the ding of the shop door opening. I jumped round, a moment of relief as I was bounding into the arms of my lover, before I realised that it wasn't him. Instead there was a stranger at the door, and three more following, and they didn't look like tourists either. Too focused, too serious. The man at the front, and a guy behind him, picked up baskets, and started stripping the shelves of high energy products; cans of beans and dried fruit. I nodded hello, but didn't bother with a smile. The third person, a woman, got an entire box of health bars and laid it at the bottom of her basket. The last one, an older man, fifty or sixty, with muscles fit for a twenty-year-old, selected the largest water containers we stocked and effortlessly carried one in each hand straight to the till.

"Hello, how are you today?" I tried to sound casual. I'd almost forgotten how to greet new people, except for tourists, who were always so keen to talk.

This man looked like he'd had a hard life of manual labour. Something like digging in fact. That must've been it; he was a quarry worker. These guys were part of the investigation team at the quarry.

Was Roj still there?

Like a swan, I bent my neck to the computer at the other end of the counter, while still managing to scan the barcode on the containers, a job I didn't really need line of sight for. I couldn't quite see the screen, so quickly took the payment, and bade him farewell so I could get back to Roj-tracking before the other investigators, who were now forming a queue, quietly demanded my attention. I moved in front of the screen, motioning the next man to wait, only to find that the screensaver had come on. I tried to tap the password, but my fingers got tangled. Shit, one more wrong entry and I'd be locked out. I felt a pair of eyes glaring at me, then another pair just beyond a basket of baked beans, sun dried tomatoes and raisins.

"Do you have some boxes we can put this stuff in?" the woman asked.

I didn't dare risk screwing-up the password entry again, and besides, I didn't want these people seeing what I was doing. If Roj was at the quarry, where he shouldn't be, he'd either be hiding or in big trouble. The last thing I should be doing was putting it up on a big screen to tell them exactly where he was.

I stepped out back and collected a few boxes. The lady helped the two guys pack their purchases, talking in a language I didn't recognise. I couldn't make out one word, which was weird because I liked to dabble in other languages to give my over-active mind something else to think about. Like recently learning sign language so I could interact with the deaf seventeen year old boy who lived on the island. But this was completely alien. Still, even though I didn't understand the words, their body language said it all. They had something to hide.

I kept quiet as I rang-through the second guy's food, the woman still putting the stuff into boxes. My immediate reaction was to feel annoyed because the woman was doing all the packing. Why was it a woman's job? But as the two guys finished, they went out to their truck and I realised we were alone. Maybe she'd engineered it that way?

I maintained silence, leaving her space to talk, but she said nothing as I scanned her purchases. Eventually I blurted out, "Can I ask what you've found?" I tried to act casual as I picked up the last of her shopping, the box of nutty bars. There was no barcode for the whole tray, so I began swiping them through one by one, even though I'd calculated the total price in one glance.

The woman opened her eyes wide. "Err, no." She sounded American, or perhaps Canadian. It must've been something serious for an international team of investigators to be flown in. I peered closely at her, hoping she'd give something away. She swung her shoulder length hair to one side so it formed a barrier between her face and the men outside. "I mean, nothing. We haven't found anything. Yet. It's just a general investigation. Actually, it's a sterile investigation." Her face was white. I tried to remember if she'd looked that pale when she came in. She certainly didn't look like she ate more than one nutty bar a day.

Half of me wanted to grab onto her skinny wrist, interrogate her about the investigation, and possibly feed her a nice bacon sandwich. But the other half needed her to leave so I could check on Roj.

"Sterile?" I asked, the word seeming out of place. "What do you mean sterile?" I imagined plastics tents, like at the end of ET, with the dead flower ET makes come back to life. The whole idea felt odd, and I had an uncomfortable feeling. And Roj. Roj was there. Right where their investigation was taking place, and he hadn't come back.

I jumped as the door dinged open again. I couldn't see the whole person, but I could tell it wasn't Roj as the skin was much fairer than his. The woman opened her mouth, but closed it again as she looked at her colleague. She picked up her now full box and knocked out a packet of dried apricots. As she leant forward to pick them up, she whispered. "I shouldn't have said sterile. It just means there is no chance of life. Sorry." And she left. Along with whoever had come to the door to fetch her.

Sorry? What was she sorry about? It was like she knew about my deepest, darkest most horrible secret, and knew there were no babies hidden in the quarry waiting to make me a mother. How could she know that? And if she didn't, what else did she mean? I didn't know whether to run after her. But say what? She'd obviously deny her little whisper if I asked her anything in front of her colleagues. And while all this was going on, where the fuck was Roj? What had they done to him? I banged my fist on the counter. The chewing gum by the till went flying into the air. All the little packets scattered across the floor.

I slid back to the keyboard, my fingers now in automatic mode typed the password in perfectly. The map appeared, but his tracking dot was no longer at the entrance to the quarry. I scanned the island for it. Nothing. It would've been easy to discard if, say, he'd been captured, it was just a wrist strap. It wasn't even waterproof. If Roj had fallen in the quarry water, or been pushed, it would just die.

My mind blanked out, not able to bear the other possibilities. They were all just scenarios. Mathematical possibilities. There was no evidence, except for Roj's absence. That was evidence. I slumped to the floor.

I heard a ding. I closed my eyes, suddenly not wanting to know, not able to stomach it being someone other than Roj. I heard someone close by, just the other side of the counter. Were they coming to get me too? I tried to breathe silently; perhaps they didn't even know I was there. Then I heard small shuffling noises, and I peered round the counter. There was Roj, squatted down in his running shorts, picking up the fallen gum packets.

My mouth agape, in my head I said, "What the fuck Roj!" but it didn't come out.

"Where have you…? How?" I gasped. Then I slapped him on the shoulder and fell into his warm body.

I could tell Roj was grinning while he stroked my hair, waiting for me to breathe normally again.

"I went to the quarry," he said.

I nodded as I looked up into his face, so glad it was in one piece. "There were lights, all the way around the rim. And loads of people, well at least twenty or thirty. More than one helo full. And loads of equipment. And you know your noise? It was even louder there."

My anxiety rose again. "I knew it, this place is evil. Even its fractal coastline is like the edge of a serrated blade."

Roj stroked my hair. "And what is it you say about fractals? It is just a pattern that keeps infinitely repeating, no matter how you look at it?" His voice was so calm and soothing. "Our life doesn't have to be like that though. We can do whatever we want. Let's say we don't have a baby; that would be okay. Or let's say we want to leave the island. That would be okay too. We can be whoever we want to be."

And at that moment, at least for a moment, at least for me, the noise stopped.

Suzi Green is a consultant, chorister and comic. Currently working on her first full-length fun fiction piece, 'Friday Night Friends', which is about four friends who have a lot of fun, a few fights and lots of …passion. Once it's finished, it'll be fantastic.

Sometimes people don't need us to care...

Machinations

Chris Foster

We all heard it. That goddamn noise. It vibrated through our feet the moment we landed in the cove. The dour captain just shrugged as if it was nothing of importance.

"It comes. It goes."

The entire two hour trip on the boat and those were the only words he uttered as we disembarked. At least he acknowledged it. The rest of the locals we met didn't. Each time it sounded they would continue unperturbed. If I asked about it, they would give me a blank look with those eyes that reminded me all too well of sharks. Inbreds. Had to be.

There weren't many mainlanders on the island. Aside from Tara, Garak and myself, there were meant to be a few others investigating the rumours of the island, of its noise, but we didn't see them. All we had seen were two honeymooners. I couldn't help myself.

"That will be us soon."

Tara looked at me as if I was an idiot before giving me a peck on the cheek.

Garak groaned. "We are here to work, Terence, remember? None of that sweetheart rubbish."

Turning, I was about to give him some witty one liner when I saw he was already half naked. Bastard spent more time in a gym than anywhere else. His Herculean body had already started tanning in the extreme summer heat as we walked to the accommodation.

Tara made a dry retching sound. "For God's sake man, at least keep your pants on."

Garak seemed to contemplate the request.

Once in our tiny room, I tried to use my tablet to bring up a map of the area while the others unpacked. Already I felt as if we were in some other dimension. The sky outside was too wide, too heavy. There were no tall buildings to hold it up, so outer space felt much closer than usual. It was unsettling. I waited impatiently for the map to load, some visual reminder that the real world was only an hour or two away. At least, if the weather calmed enough. At this rate the winds looked to prevent any return to the mainland for six months. I didn't like the idea of staying here more than a day.

"Think of the contract like this: it's not a marriage, just a prolonged fling with someone in between."

Trust Tara to think like that when I had objected to the trip. She constantly referred to relationship metaphors to explain things. This contract, wanting a puppy, even deciding what to have for dinner. This time she won out. We were being paid overtime, more than enough to logically rationalise away any unsettled feelings I may have had about working on an island only two hours away from the mainland.

"It'll be just like Tasmania!"

It was nothing like Tasmania. Our wedding was to be in winter, up in Cataract Gorge just outside of Launceston. We had been there once. Car was encased in ice by the morning. She liked the cold. I didn't, but I liked her. Another reason why I was on this stupid island right now – a happy Tara meant a happy me.

"Right we are. No wifi," I said with a grumble, "no reception on my phone and the ruggedized sat mobile from the company has no data. We'll have to rely on the pdfs for maps."

Garak *pffted*. "We're here to investigate the noise, ensure the quarry is safe and get a tan. We know, we know."

He didn't notice my eyeroll. It seemed a simple job. Hell, it almost seemed a responsible job, especially for a company known for profits before people. What didn't make sense was why we had to check the quarry was safe *now*. Twenty years had passed since it last operated. There were rumours on the internal company channels that an ex-worker had gone mad and slaughtered his family last week, proclaiming loudly about the noise of the quarry finding him again. He was now suing the company in a private legal battle, helped along by his therapist, lawyer, cactus plant and hospital nurse. Of course, this was said with other water cooler gossip, such as the CEO being a pornstar in her spare time and the IT department hacking everyone's accounts so they can establish their own criminal syndicate. All possible, but never taken seriously.

I flicked through the history pages of the report and found a more detailed account of the island's first settlers. They had sailed on the largest, most advanced ship ever built – or so the literature read. Of course when it became a shipwreck, it mysteriously disappeared, probably lost to the sea and found only in old tales from ancient story spinners.

Note to self, find out who writes our company reports and pass on his details to a publishing house. Then contact HR.

More recent history made a passing reference to a noise. I wondered once again what had happened twenty years ago. The quarry ran out of stone. Simple. Except that couldn't be all. Everything suggested there were still profits to be made. Then this noise, whatever it was, had started to appear in the report. No explanation. No reason. No recognition it was there at all. Even the company reporter, with all his flairs for first settlers and churning weather reports, only ever made singular references – *Noise heard.* End of story.

"Nothing helpful so far, anyone else want to read the rest of this report?"

Tara pretended not to hear me and Garak was doing squats, his counting rising in volume.

Guess not.

The table of contents listed 'anecdotal records' appended to the back of the report. I hadn't bothered with them before now. After all, what would they say? Worker looked in quarry. Said, 'No stone.'

No, I'd had other things on my mind like our wedding and how on earth I was going to accommodate the growing list of people Tara knew. Whoever in the company had made this pdf had done a fine job, though, even providing links to each chapter from the table of contents. Except for the anecdotal records. That link was broken.

Frustration and mild nausea from being on a boat for two hours brewed in me. Going to the previous chapter I scrolled down until I found the records. I saw a red annotation at the start, noting that these records were 'commercial in confidence' and not to be shared, then came a summary: the workers had heard a noise, likely the same noise I now had the displeasure of hearing; half of them, the fly-in fly-out workers, seemed to lose their minds on hearing it; then they all disappeared, never to be seen again.

"What rot."

I shook my head. It made no sense. The records were sketchy. Some were so far-fetched I wondered if whoever had written the report thought he would have some fun with the story and added fictional records at the back. After all, tiny island, closed quarry, who would ever read all this?

Gritting my teeth, I kept reading through the records themselves now.

The first one said something about the men, driven mad by the sound, running as deep as the tunnels allowed.

Hang on, tunnels? It's a quarry, there aren't any tunnels.

Frustrated at the writer's preference for storytelling over facts, I looked through the jumbled record. Some reference was made to caves south of the quarry, on the coast, and that these might connect to a network of caves below the island through natural watercourses. Perhaps twenty years ago this had been just a possibility. Now we had geo-technology to prove it one way or another.

Another record then made mention of ghosts in the caves. A worker from overseas deigned to say anything about ghosts. A brief moment of sanity took me before I read on and saw that she was rebuking the ghost story because it was clearly a demon, who growled like a storm and shrieked like a banshee.

If anything even remotely close to these records ever happened it was only in the writer's mind, while he took a particularly strong dose of acid after reading one too many Stephen King novels.

Still, at least we had a lead. All records, fictional or otherwise, mentioned the noise being loudest around the caves south of the quarry along the coast. It was possible that natural watercourses under the quarry had carried that sound to the worksite.

"Yo bookworm, when is Squirrel turning up?" Garak was now doing handstand push ups against the wall. Clearly his methods of passing time were different to mine.

Tara was staring absently at Garak, probably mentally reorganising the table arrangements for the wedding for the umpteenth time. I hoped.

"Show some respect, Garak," It sounded like I was being a pompous ass but I was wary enough of this island without possibly insulting the one contact we had. "His name is Dr Larwskon. He should be here any minute. Hopefully he'll be able to shed some light on all these ghost stories."

"Wait, what?"

I waved the tablet at him with the last record on-screen. Garak knew everything there was to know about rocks. Reading reports on the other hand...

"Ghosts and demons and mad men, oh my!" I said with my

best Dorothy impression from 'The Wizard of Oz'. "The caves are haunted. That's why the quarry shut. Sounds like we might have to go check it out."

His eyes widened and he paused, sweat trickling off his upside down face. "Nah mate, you're pulling my leg."

Before we could say anything else the noise hit us, deep vibrations mixed with something so high pitched I felt it in my head instead of with my ears. The tablet screen flickered briefly. Garak curled forward before standing upright jerkily. Then silence, glorious silence. Until there was a knock at the door.

It was Squirrel, an old codename for Dr Bennifer Larwskon, a weedy scientist who was born and raised on the island. I had met him once before at company headquarters. He was a strange man, who had worn a lab coat despite the Australian summer. Even now in this tropical heat he was wearing a tattered white lab coat. Lord knows how he practised science from here. This place had a town shaman for crying out loud.

"Tara, Garak, *Terence*." The way he said my name let me know quite clearly he remembered me. We hadn't parted favourably. "As I said to the company, there really is no need for outside interference. The quarry is empty of stone, full of water. What else do they want to know?"

"Happy to meet you too, Bennifer," said Tara, flashing him a smile.

"It's Doctor Larwskon, if you mind. The island is functioning well. Research is good. Again, why are you here?" His nervous twitching reminded me of his codename. Highly original.

My main concern was he seemed a few nuts short of a winter harvest. The island was functioning well? What were we, council planners? I tried to keep the impatience out of my voice. After all, I had already insulated him once back on the mainland, no need to start a fight on his home soil. "I am glad your research is going well Dr. Larwskon, but the company heard reports from multiple tourists that there was a strange noise emanating from near the quarry. As our brief explained, we're here to make sure the quarry is stable and not collapsing underground. There's not exactly a lot of island to begin with."

Garak pulled his arms back and turned his chest in a stretch, rolling his eyes at us.

"No local has reported any–" As Squirrel spoke the noise sounded again, deep vibrations that set my teeth on edge. "–noise complaints and my seismograph has detected no abnormal seismic activity."

"Doctor, are you honestly telling me you didn't just hear that?"

"Maybe it's the ghosts," teased Tara.

"Or angry B&B hosts lamenting their lack of guests?" goaded Garak.

Garak and Tara smiled at each other.

Dr. Larwskon glared at Tara. "If you are so intent on seeing things for yourself, I suggest you, Miss Tara, accompany me down to Quarry Lake right now. I have a two-man kayak. As the company has stressed to me you must write the report for your," he paused to glare at me, "*team leader* to sign, the sooner we go, the sooner this operation of fruitlessness can be over. We've got all sorts coming to check things out later today, you might as well be the first. Won't take long, the lake is a lot smaller than what you envisage. You two can go walk around, make yourselves useless." With that he stormed away.

With a quick look of surprise, Tara gave me a kiss and a wink. "Told you this would be fun! I order the two of you to have brunch. Then find out what you can about the island, by any means necessary, tour guides included. Later we get to go hunt some ghosts!" Away she went after him.

"Yeah. Fun." I turned to ask Garak what he wanted to do but saw he was already headed out of the door.

"C'mon! Paid business trip! Woo hoo!"

His enthusiasm brought a smile to my face. Why not? There had to be something to do in this town.

There was nothing to do in Amama Harbour. Even Garak seemed a little subdued at the prospects: whale watching, cave paintings or land-crab migration. Having spent two hours on a boat in seas turning sour for the season, the idea of looking at more water didn't thrill either of us. Instead we went up the road to the community centre for a counter meal. It had a bar and a deck overlooking the harbour.

"Thirty-seven dollars for a burger? Without chips! It's cheaper in Sydney!"

The plump woman behind the bar stared at me, black eyes unblinking. One side of her mouth slid up. I presume it was meant to be a smile. Time was passing, slowly, long enough for the silence to become awkward. Then with the slow delivery of a prime minister declaring war she spoke with the coarsest voice I had ever heard. "Try. Sydney. Then." The other side of her mouth slid up, so smooth a movement for such a wide face I considered for one fanciful moment there was machinery beneath her skin moving her lips on a pulley system.

Some of the locals were murmuring behind us, about how we should go back to the mainland if we didn't like it here, how Jane liked it here, how people left if they didn't, like Michael and Archie – they left. It didn't sound like Michael or Archie would be returning either.

One, an old woman with an eye tattoo and teeth like a sugar drinker, smiled at me and mouthed something. *Fate? Bait? Late?* I never could read lips.

Once again that noise went through the place. My teeth clamped and I bit the side of my tongue. Pain, sharp and intense, cut at my attention as if I had licked the edge of a knife.

Of course the woman behind the counter showed no reaction.

I didn't bother to ask if she heard it. Instead I spoke to Garak. "What do you think, split it fifty fifty?"

Garak didn't reply. His head was twitching repetitively. Everyone was staring. Their solemn faces almost showed sympathy.

"Garak? Garak!" I grabbed his shoulder and gripped it tight.

With a jolt he stopped twitching and looked around as if concussed. "All hands on deck."

"What?"

"Engines below capacity."

"What?"

He seemed to notice me for the first time. "What?"

"Are you okay?"

He wiped his hand over his face. The woman behind the bar muttered something and went back to her muted conversation with a young man further down the counter. Some of the locals left, their meals unfinished. Scratching his chest, Garak looked at me with the closest thing to seriousness I had ever seen on the man's face. "I'm buying two burgers. You get what you want. Charge it to the company. Then I'm finding out what's making that damn noise."

Nodding in agreement, I thought it was the best idea he'd had all day.

We declined the offer of a guide and decided to follow a map to the southern caves and their apparent cave paintings. Unsurprisingly, the brochure mentioned nothing about possible habitant ghosts or demons.

At least we're finding out what we can about the island.

The track would take us past the quarry so I could check on Tara too. An hour or so had passed since Tara went off with the Squirrel and I hadn't heard a word from her. Checking my phone for the umpteenth time, I found it was the same as ever – full signal, zero messages. The company had provided us with sat phones in case of emergency. I should have been relieved that Tara hadn't used it.

Sighing to myself, I tried to shake off the feeling of unease. Something didn't sit right. Bennifer didn't exactly strike confidence in me either. How big was Quarry Lake? Could they drown? Why didn't he organise to meet us all in his office?

And what was with the ghost stories?

I was so distracted by my thoughts I almost didn't notice that Garak was wearing budgie smugglers. He trotted past me with a shovel over his shoulder, gave a curt nod and kept going, head bobbing in time to a song only he could hear. I just managed to catch him grunt something about the noise.

"Hey, we're headed for caves, remember? I'll just grab some water."

He kept going.

Half an hour later, I was drenched and still hadn't caught up with Garak. The man wasn't even in sight. How he managed to move so fast when the heat was dictator level oppressive was beyond me. Luckily I didn't have to stay too alert to find the quarry – Quarry Road led straight to it. Its edges were trimmed with overgrown forest. Shadows interweaved across the ground, providing brief respites from the sun but not the heat. For a moment I felt like Indiana Jones exploring some mystical ruin nestled in an exotic jungle. Unfortunately the only real similarity was the humidity. I crossed the wide space to the lake's edge, my legs unbalanced from their rigorous use.

Squirrel was right, the lake is small.

The ultra vibrant aqua and teal hues of the lake were mesmerising. I knew the colours were enhanced by the rare minerals that would have been disturbed when the quarry was functioning. The water was also probably incredibly treacherous. Often quarry lakes were as cold as ice and filled with forgotten pieces of machinery – metal rods, wiring, scaffolding – there were a dozen dangers that made the idyllic-looking scene a possible death trap beneath the vibrant blue.

Across the liquid surface a cool breeze rolled like a draft under a door. I wiped the sweat from my brow and drank from my water bottle. The plastic had flavoured the water in the heat and I was tempted to drink from the lake. My knowledge of the heavy metals likely swirling in the water stopped me. Plastic or metal. Man made vs natural. Both deadly in the long run.

Looking over the water, I tried to see the shape of a kayak over near the far quarry wall but there was nothing. Against the glare of the blue sky and the sun's reflected light, it glistened as bright as fire. My eyes burned when I tried to look from this angle.

Odd. No Tara. No Squirrel. Not even Garak.

A feeling of being watched descended on me. Around the top edge of the quarry, movement caught my eye. When I looked, all I saw was the forest, overgrown and swaying in what little breeze there was. The trees groaned, their sound metallic. An unsettled feeling filled my gut. If Tara and Squirrel weren't here, then where were they? Had something happened?

Breathe. Relax. This is what Tara is always going on about. 'You think the bride has bolted just because she needed the bathroom on the way to the chapel.'

A deep breath. One two three, one two three...

The noise sounded again, louder and closer than before. It went right through me, my jaw locking shut with pain and nerves aching. The water swirled as if disturbed by some great beast beneath the surface. I turned and made my way back to Quarry Road as fast as I could.

By the time I reached it again, the water had resumed its placid serenity. Teal and aqua shades rippled gently with the lazy breeze. Far up on the rim among the heat waves there may have been a group of figures. None of them seemed fit enough to be Garak. Tara wasn't there either. In the distance I heard what may have been helicopters.

I turned continued down Quarry Road towards the caves.

I followed the road, eventually reaching a weathered sign post that said: 'South Point' and 'White Beach'. A quick check of the map suggested that, unless I wanted to prolong the foolishness of walking in temperatures high enough to fry the bacon as well as the eggs, I should follow the sign.

The path took me through more jungle. Unlike Quarry Road, which had been mostly limestone and hard earth, this trek was far more natural. Sweat soaked through my clothes, thunder rumbled in the distance and more than once I stumbled through spiderwebs of a much stronger ilk than back home. Repeatedly, I thought I glimpsed someone else, only to see nothing but steamy heat when I focused.

It was while trying to disengage from a particularly large web that the noise struck again. I felt it travel through the ground like a snake in the wall. My ears clenched internally as if on a plane and my thoughts sparked with images of pistons pumping life into some complicated machine. My breath caught and my body froze. There was something unnatural about the sound. If not for the creator of the thick web that suddenly scurried across my arm, I may have stayed standing still long after the noise ended.

After what felt like hours of continued walking, the scenery changed. The trees seemed to thin marginally. There was a tang in the air. I checked my watch and believed it to be lying when it showed little more than thirty minutes had gone by. Instead of arguing I plodded forward, one foot then another. Finally the trees parted and I was slapped in the face by a strong salty breeze. The ocean stretched out before me, turbulent grey slabs shifting like the slow pulse of an apex predator. Far below I could see White Beach. Nestled between the water and I were cliffs pockmarked with cave entrances. Across the water, thick clouds rolled ever closer, white tears ripping at them as lightning jumped.

"Well now, which cave has the paintings and which has the ghosts?" I mumbled to myself. "Eeny meeny miney moe…"

By the time I reached the cave I'd selected, I saw it was nothing more than a cleft in the cliff. It barely seemed noteworthy, more like an accidental fissure that cracked during a wild Pacific storm.

"Garak! Tara! You two in here?"

No reply.

Don't jump to conclusions. Check the paintings, see if there are any tunnels, and get the hell back to Amama Harbour before that storm hits.

As if to confirm my thoughts, deep rumbling filled the cave. I glanced outside and saw the storm had already halved the distance between us. Ducking back into the cave I found the paintings. They looked like rust stains and nothing more.

Grunting with disappointment, I checked the brochure, which contained amazingly detailed images of space ships, animals, tribal signs and tribal people. The backstory of the original settlers surrounded the pictures, filled with tales of the shipwrecked crew.

Then I noticed the tiny fine print beneath the photos that looked nothing like the cliff:

*Artist impression overlaid on image.

Looking at the rust stains once more, I grimaced. It would take a lot of acid to get such wonderful impressions from this.

I checked the sat phone once more and was surprised to see I had no reception. A message on the phone's screen helpfully warned that no calls could be made. Delightful.

A sound, like a sharp intake of breath, gusted past me.

I looked up, expecting to see another face, but there was no one and nothing around. The temperature was rapidly dropping and I was the wrong side of the island for shelter. But in the cleft there was a small bend and shadow. Desperate to get out of the elements, at least for a moment to think, I squeezed my way into the gap. My back pressed against hard stone... only to find the rock behind me bent.

"What the..."

There was a loud crack and the rock fell away, an eye of darkness appearing in its place. Unable to catch myself in time I fell with it, swallowed by the dark. Something sharp cut at my calves and cold, moist air clogged my lungs.

"Damn!"

Once upright again, I flicked on my phone's torchlight. I was in a new part of the cave. Water trickled around my feet and headed further into the darkness. The space was small but seemed to be a tunnel leading back towards the quarry. The walls were slick with wet, my torch catching the light. I picked up the 'rock' that had collapsed inward and noticed the back of it was metal.

"That's weird."

Upon closer inspection, what I had thought was some sort of stone was in fact a metal sheet covered with several layers of salt air grime. Garak would have laughed at my mistake. Right now, I wished he would.

Where is that walking mountain anyway?

Among the pearlescent glistenings on the walls seemed to be pictures. Pictures of...

Squinting, I leaned closer. A crack in the cliff wall gave the impression of a biohazard sign. Next to it was something that almost looked like an old health warning, the kind plastered around the company's worksites and large vehicles. Of course such a sign here would be impossible, as these 'cave' paintings had been here since the earliest settlers on the island generations ago.

A metallic tapping sound caught my attention. It was coming from further down the tunnel.

Knock knock, who's there?

Despite the coming storm I pressed forward. With each step the tunnel seemed to narrow, sharp turns and low ceilings making the trek a tight squeeze. My feet were getting wetter and I realised that the water was now ankle-deep. I turned another corner and entered a wide open cavern.

The noise blasted me. It wailed like a shrieking banshee. The air vibrated with the force of it. Its echoes bounced off the hard surfaces in a clashing medley of primal rage. It was so much stronger now, louder, fiercer. Horrific creatures from the realm of nightmares clung to the walls, multi-limbed and of behemoth proportions. I fell back, heart hammering against my chest. My phone slipped from my grasp, its light sending shadows leaping and dashing as it fell into the water.

The noise stopped, leaving only echoes to replay softer and softer until they become little more than manic whispers.

Unable to move, fear paralyzed me. Years passed between each heartbeat. Adrenaline flooded my body and every subtle sound had me recall all the things in my life that had ever seemed similar. Slowly, ever so slowly, my breath returned and to my surprise no teeth, talon, claw or maw harmed me.

Crawling to the bobbing light of my phone, I avoided looking directly at it. The tapping sound from earlier was louder, more rapid now. Shielding my eyes, I reached out and grabbed the phone.

Except the light stayed bobbing in the water.

"What…"

Tapping the button on the side the phone in my hand, it sprang to life. It was identical to mine – except it wasn't. It was Tara's.

"Tara!"

Hitting its flashlight, I quickly checked the area. The 'monsters' were nothing more than odd rock formations. The cavern didn't appear to lead anywhere. Water pooled in a shallow pond in the centre. The water seemed different but I couldn't quite discern why.

It was translucent, the pond bed only knee-deep. There was no sign of Tara. I picked up my phone and dual-wielded the torchlights in case I had missed something.

Nothing. Except for creepy rock formations, the area was empty.

Quickly I checked my freshly acquired mobile for messages. The phone's outbox had two drafts that had failed to send – both of which had been addressed to my number:

Squirrel's weird. Love you. See you at the caves.

That was typical of Tara. Combining two unrelated thoughts into one short message. And it confirmed she was coming here. So where was she?

The next message was not like her:

Quarry bad! Tunnels. Evac asap.

My breath caught and sweat that had nothing to do with the heat, chilled me. What was wrong with the quarry? Tara was always brief in her messages and not for the first time I wish she had said more. An evacuation? She was never one to cause alarm. An eye roll and shake of the head, that's what she would do if she were here – plus some flippant comment about so-and-so being a worry wart. That was the Tara I knew. Not '*Evac asap*'.

As I hurried back up the tunnel, another thought hit me. Did she mean for us to evac the island as quickly as time allowed, or did she mean the danger was immediate and that time had already run dry? Either way, it meant whatever was happening was imminent. I had to find her.

On my way back to the quarry, the storm started swallowing the sky. Light dulled with the coming evening while thunder grumbled constantly and seemed to steal the air. Twice as I ran the noise struck again, as if roaring a challenge to the storm. Each pulse of sound vibrated through the earth and split the air. I took a chance and raced through the jungle in what I thought was a short cut. Ridges of white limestone reflected the last of the heat along the path. Spindly trees cast little more than slithers of shadow in the remaining light. Instead of arriving at Quarry Road I ended up overlooking the ocean once more.

My scream was drowned out by the storm and the noise as they clashed once again. I slipped and fell towards some of the caves I hadn't explored earlier. When I rose, I saw Garak atop the cliffs. Relief hit me harder than the noise. With his help we would be able to get a rescue team together. I ran over.

His head was barely above ground. He was deep in a hole, digging into the dirt. I called to him to stop. He ignored me. Even showing him Tara's phone couldn't distract him from his task, his eyes set firmly in the deepening pit.

"Garak! Leave it alone! We have to go find…"

"It's down there. I know it! Just a little further. Just a bit deeper. I'll find it, you'll see. I'll find that goddamn noise and catch it and break it."

I feared the sun had addled his brain. If it had been Tara, or indeed anyone other than a six-foot-four herculean figure with a shovel in hand, I would have physically grabbed and hauled them back to shelter. My heart broke as I realised he had lost the plot. He was of no help. In fact he was acting just like the records had described quarry workers twenty years ago…

He was also a long way down, hitting the shovel against something metallic. In the darkening light he looked like a fairy tale monster, ready to steal children and drag them into the darkness. Then he barked. Or was it laughter?

Garak looked up with a grin on his face. "I found it, I found the noise!"

My heart skipped a beat. The man had completely lost his mind in the space of a few hours. Yet part of me wanted to know, wanted to *believe*. Because if Garak had found the noise, then it was possible Tara might be nearby.

Garak swung the shovel over his head and slammed it down on the metal. The clanging was loud and brutal. After a couple of hits, the sound changed, like the metal was bending. Finally there was a rending noise that conjured images of rusty sheet metal being torn.

That's when the noise decided to come back, this time louder and stronger.

I fell to my knees, almost tumbling into Garak's pit. My teeth felt as if they wanted to shatter, so tight was my jaw. Nerves throughout my face constricted and never had I felt so much pain from a sound. I was unable to open my eyes but heard Garak cry out, blasted by the noise through whatever hole he had made. It reverberated through the ground, shaking loose the soil surrounding Garak.

I forced my eyes open. The sound started to recede, but with it I heard Tara's cry. She was screaming, her voice tinny and seeming to come from the other side of Garak's metallic discovery.

But the hole was collapsing.

Thunder rumbled and fat drops of rain began to spit at us. Dirt was falling, plugging the opening, dampening into mud. All the while Garak was screaming berserk, clawing at the metal with his bare hands as soil filled up around him.

"Tara! Garak!"

I slid into the hole, grabbed half of the submerged shovel, and tried to fling the dirt back out. Garak had dug too deep and no matter how fast I shovelled the soil was raining back down on us. There was only one alternative.

"Out of the way, Garak!"

He didn't hear me and there was no time to argue. I stabbed the shovel into the hole, trying to widen whatever gap Garak had made. Already we were buried up to our knees. Each layer of soil was making it harder to hit effectively. The rain became heavier. Suddenly the hole illuminated. Above us someone was holding a torch by the edge of the pit.

"Hey! Help! Throw us a rope or something! Help!"

The torch light blinded my eyes and I felt more dirt come tumbling down, faster than before.

"Hey! Stop! We're down here!"

Whoever was above seemed to be pushing the dirt mounds on top of us. Garak took a deep breath and dived under the loose soil. He was submerged in seconds.

Panic took over as I slammed the shovel one last time between my feet, praying to a god I rarely thought of that I didn't hit Garak. I felt the spade's edge bite something hard, its head push through, and suddenly the ground gave way. Garak writhed under me before disappearing. A moment later I fell too, my hands scrambling to try holding something. Sharp metal clawed into me and I squirmed trying to avoid the worst of it. I was stuck, suffocating and barely able to move my arms. Mud covered my face. Something roared above me, possibly thunder. Something shifted below and I felt metal teeth scrape away most of my side.

I always wanted to lose my lovehandles.

The pain replaced all thoughts. I fell properly this time, hitting hard ground. Dirt fell on top of me but, no longer confined to a narrow dug out, it trailed off to the sides. Screaming echoes sounded around me and then I realised it was my voice. In the dark it was hard to see anything.

A bright beam illuminated the space. The hulking back of Garak was highlighted. His shape crawled away, a dark smear left behind like a nightmarish snail. Turning, I saw Tara crumpled against a wall, her face bloodied, holding a torch.

"Told you to evac." Her voice was hoarse.

I tried to reach out to her but the pain was too much. I looked around, saw the reinforced walls, ceiling. We were in a tunnel. A man-made tunnel. I groaned.

The air was stuffy. Somewhere there was a sound. It was emanating from further down the tunnel, in Garak's direction.

Somehow I dragged myself to Tara's side. We held hands and looked into the darkness, her torch switched off.

After a while I noticed a dim glow in Garak's direction.

It was getting harder to breathe.

"Squirrel's weird. Love You." Tara coughed. I think she tried to laugh.

"He *is* weird. I love you too. Even if you never listen to my instructions."

Her head nestled against my chest. A rumble started and the noise, that goddamn noise, hit us. She went rigid, like I had, and her teeth smashed together as our jaws locked. I felt like my eardrums would burst. It was stronger again, louder, more thunderous and more high pitched. The torch flickered to life under the strain of the noise. The far wall illuminated briefly, bones littered on the ground. Barely legible rusty signs adorned the wall above them and suddenly I got it.

I tried to laugh but cried instead. Pain was sawing through me as if I was still being dragged through the hole above us. "I get it. I know what that noise is!"

Tears streamed down my face. My head was light, from blood loss or lack of oxygen I didn't know. I didn't care. I felt Tara's tears on my chest.

"I know. I know too."

We held each other, the noise shuddering through us. My eyes gazed longingly at where the exit should be. Fallen rock impossibly thick filled the space from floor to ceiling.

"I think we should call our first boy George." My voice was light. I could see George, wearing little overalls. "And raise him on acreage, with lots of ducks. I always liked ducks."

Tara's voice was a murmur against my chest. Above us the dirt stopped falling so heavily through the hole. There was a thickness in the air. I felt like it was smothering me. Clicking and whirling could be heard, the sounds faint and mechanic.

Somewhere down the tunnel Garak roared.

Chris Foster is an award winning poet & novelist living in Australia. Despite lacking the necessary cat and caffeine addiction, he is completely passionate about writing and continues to produce books at every opportunity. He also loves fishing, gaming, making others smile, the occasional road trip and people who know the difference between there/their/they're. He also blogs haphazardly at www.chrisfosterwrites.com

Sometimes we need to escape caring...

Escape

Alexandra Cain

11am. Nine hours to go

I hear they're talking to people. Asking them about the noise. Locals are swarming around the community centre, desperate as always to talk.

When I first agreed to move here, it was for peace and quiet, to get my head straight after everything that'd happened back home. Away from London traffic, from the big city crush of people. Solitude and time to think, I thought. Teaching some sweet, innocent island kids.

"Ahh, you're that English lass who's going to be the new teacher," said a fat, white-haired man, as soon as I boarded that rust-riddled excuse for a boat and headed out to the island.

So yeah, I was wrong. Stupidly, blindly, only-Jane-could-be-that-much-of-an-idiot wrong. Because it turns out I could've walked through central London wearing nothing but a hat and I would've attracted less attention than on the island. Privacy? No. Everyone on this isolated rock knows more about my business than the people I worked with at that London school for four years. And now, with the noise, peace and quiet is completely out of reach.

I should have left already, but it's obvious why I've stayed, in fact it's almost embarrassing – I stayed for a man. In my case, rather than being for a typical tall, dark handsome man, it's for a short-ish, blonde-haired ex-investment banker by the name of Dan, a little too obsessed with computer games, Formula One racing and bacon sandwiches.

The island's lack of privacy is the reason I've been nervous, especially since I heard about the noise investigation. Too many people getting right up in other people's business on this island.

12 noon. Eight hours to go

I have a song stuck in my head, *Hey Jude*, which is a strange choice given my current mood. The soothing na na na na-na-na-naa chorus rises and falls rhythmically in my head, clashing with the jitters in my stomach.

I'm lounging around Dan's cottage when the phone rings.

"Hi Jane, how's it going?" It's Leanne, the girl who works part-time in Minna and Roj's shop. I struck up a kind of friendship with her when I first arrived, but she started to annoy me with her constant, self-appointed therapist-type questions, so I pushed her away. Nowadays, she's an interesting, if sometimes unreliable, source of gossip.

"I'm fine."

"Hey, heard they're going to dredge the quarry?"

What? They can't. If they dredge the quarry, my secret might get discovered and I can't have that yet. Not yet. My stomach lurches, so I thank Leanne and slam the phone down.

Na na na na-na-na-naa…

I sit on the couch, trying to calm myself, focusing on the mould that curls around the left-hand corner of the living room wall in the shape of South America. Dan and I fought so many times about this derelict cottage. I once dreamed of a newly-built, dry place down near the harbour, but this is Dan's old family home and he didn't want to move. It wasn't a bad house in its day, by island standards. A strong, brick base. Thick, wooden panels painted white. It's isolated, further away from the harbour than most of the rest of the island's dwellings, closer to the quarry. I like that the winds aren't as fierce here, and I've come to value solitude over convenience. Particularly in light of recent events.

As I stare at the mould, my mind drifts back to the first time I heard the noise that now comes regularly from the quarry. I was sitting in this exact position, except it was the middle of winter and the dead of night. Only my face and one arm stuck out of a thick, woollen blanket. I was attempting to calm my insomniac brain by sipping a cuppa made from my second-to-last bag of peppermint tea, wondering whether to dry the bag and use it again. I'm the only one on the island that buys it, apart from the occasional tourist, so Minna from the shop never orders enough, no matter how many times I ask. She hates me, like most people on this island seem to.

I sat there, listening to that rhythmic, almost sing-song sound. Then I realised. The noise was saying my name. Jane, Jane, Jane. It was Morgan's voice, calling to me. From the other side of the world, from another life. Morgan, my beautiful twin sister. Non-identical.

I'd shrugged off the blanket and grabbed a cigarette, hands shaking so hard it took me a few attempts to light. Then, I'd poured myself a large glass of straight gin.

After that night, I discovered I was not the only one on the island who had heard the noise. But I'm the only one who knows what it says.

And why.

1pm. Seven hours to go

Another hour gone, but many still left. I'm waiting until it's dark, which I reckon will be about 8pm. Then it will be safe to escape the island, take a boat to the mainland where I'll be able to keep my secrets safe. I can't sit here all day. But where can I go until it's time?

I get up off the couch and turn away from the mould, away from happier memories of Dan and I, towards the liquor cabinet. There's enough gin left for one glass. I knock it back straight, not even bothering to get ice. What have I got left? A little bourbon. And the tequila, if I'm desperate, even though I can't stand the taste. Still, that might be better than having to see Minna's face if I go to buy some more.

Dan and I are very similar people, perhaps too similar. Too bitter, too miserable. I wasn't always that way. Yet, I can't blame Dan for the change; it began long before I met him.

Na na na na-na-na-naa...

The noise echoes again; Jane, Jane Jane. Morgan had so many voices – when she wanted something, when angry, when excited. Right now, the noise sounds like her happy voice and it takes me back to the summer when she visited me in Granada, Spain, where I was studying for six months during my final year of university. I was having the time of my life, but I was still happy to see Morgan's familiar, beautiful face. It was the longest we had ever been apart.

"Bloody hell, Jane, you look great. The blonde suits you. And you've lost so much weight."

For the first few days, we had a great time. One night, I took her to a tapas bar – "the food is actually free, wow" – where we met two Aussie backpackers. Jon was a charming journalist with shaggy brown hair and beautiful green eyes, while his friend Scott was a pale, doughy accountant. We fell into the usual pattern, where it was assumed that I would be lumped with the boy that neither of us wanted. Yet, it didn't take long for me to notice that it was my words Jon was latching onto, my hand that he took playfully. Me. As the night wound on we both realised that for once she was not the obviously most attractive, most likeable sister. Things had changed.

After I finished university, I got a teaching job at a school in London and Morgan and I shared a tiny, run-down flat in Hammersmith. I had the only bedroom because I paid most of the rent, and Morgan, who had a steady stream of jobs – hairdressing apprentice, florist, promotions girl, stripper – slept on a sort of landing area outside my bedroom. The early days were fun, and our flat was always full of friends, but Morgan's behaviour became increasingly erratic. She would borrow large sums of money off me, then go out on payday and party all her earnings away, or buy expensive clothes and trinkets.

Looking back, I should have seen the signs of substance abuse. Perhaps I did know and didn't want to believe. It was easy enough to explain away: surely she was just a girl who liked to party? A girl who had always been thin, and had just become a little gaunt? Sure, her face was a bit pale and hollow, but it was winter in London.

The friends began to drift away, save a few dodgy-looking hangers-on, and Morgan moped around by herself, miserable and annoying. I began to feel like I was trapped in a bad marriage, and I was more concerned with how and if I would ever make it out and carry on with my life.

It all came to a head one night when I was at home alone, or so I thought. I had just cooked dinner and was looking in the cupboard for the little box of hot sauces Morgan had given me for Christmas.

"I took them away," her voice said from behind me, making me jump.

"I didn't know you were home."

She looked at me, short dark hair unwashed and sticking out, her chin jutted; that contrary look which meant she was wanting a fight. I was determined not to give her the satisfaction.

"I took them away. The sauces. You didn't deserve them because you were mean to me," Morgan said. Her voice was sing-song, child-like.

Mean? You're hundreds of pounds in debt to me and you take away the crappy £5 present you gave me. Screw you!!! But I managed to say nothing and walk away.

She followed me. "See, Jane, you can't go being mean to me and not inviting me out with your friends. You thought you'd gotten away with it, sneaking out in your new mini skirt."

I finally burst. "Don't be bloody stupid. It was someone's birthday at work."

"Don't lie to me smarty pants. I saw your phone. It's those new friends of yours. You never invite me anywhere."

"I don't have to invite you everywhere! And why did you have my phone anyway?"

"You're embarrassed to be seen with me. It's because I'm a stripper, isn't it?"

"No, Morgan, it's because you're miserable. You used to be fun and you didn't need me to look after you."

"You're a bitch, Jane. You're the one who's changed. You used to be a nice person."

"Well, Morgan, you've always been a bitch. And I don't want to live with you anymore. Get out!"

I ran to her landing bedroom and picked up a big handful of clothes, then opened the front door and threw them into the hallway.

Morgan started crying. "Please, Jane no. I didn't mean it. I swear. I'm sorry."

"Just go."

She whimpered and shuffled off, returning a few minutes later with a duffle bag. "Bye, Jane. I'm really going now."

"I'll send the rest of your stuff home to Mum and Dad." I went into my room, slammed the door, and turned on music.

"Janey, Janey," her voice called at the door. "I really, really need your help. I'm not well."

I turned up the music and didn't come out of my room for three hours. By then, she was gone.

2pm. Six hours to go

I decide to get out of Dan's cottage and hike up to the quarry. Perhaps I'll be able to see what the investigators are doing. Take my mind off my secrets, my sister, dredging, escape. Make the hours move faster.

It's hot and I'm unfit from lazing around, and from the cigarettes, so I don't know if I'll make it. Still, it's better than doing nothing.

I start, slowly, through the bushland track behind the house, which is thick with tall eucalyptus trees and damp with leaves and mulch that never see much sunlight.

I'm used to the landscape now. It was all so foreign when I came here, straight from working in a London primary school that fed into a high school where there were stabbings every week. Sick of kids with hard attitudes and tough mouths, I imagined myself skipping along, *Sound of Music*-style holding the hands of island kids. But when I arrived at that one-room school down by the harbour, I found the kids no more welcoming than in London. In fact, it wasn't long before I was planning to leave again.

Then I met Dan. I was attracted to him the moment I met him – his intelligence, his sarcastic sense of humour. His dad had sent him away to boarding school on the mainland, to get him a good career. And he succeeded. It's hard to look at Dan, sitting around in his tracksuit bottoms playing computer games, and think him a success, but he was once a high-flying investment banker. He made a decent amount of money too, but burned out at thirty-five from the pressure and ended up moving back here. He has a bit of cash left, probably not enough to live off forever but for a few years at least. And his parents and only sibling, Mary, died in a boating accident while he was away, so he inherited their cottage, run down as it is.

He's stuck in a weird no-man's land, where he's classified as a local but still an outsider. I suspect it's also to do with the reason Dan's dad got the cash to send him away – some shady deal around the quarry, I think, before it shut down. Not even Dan knows the full story.

The noise calls as I near the quarry and it's Morgan again. Jane, Jane, Jane.

Of course, that story didn't end well. My parents contacted me a few weeks after the night Morgan and I fought. I was surprised to find she hadn't gone back to their house as I assumed she would. We started looking for her and eventually my parents found her. In a morgue.

I went to the funeral, or at least I tried. My father turned me away at the entrance to the chapel.

"Please, Dad, I really want to say goodbye to Morgan."

"If you hadn't turned her out on the street none of us would be saying goodbye to her." His handsome, lined face was twisted with disgust.

"But, it wasn't like that. I didn't know what she was up to… and she was so difficult."

"I know she was, but she was your sister and if you'd looked after her then she never would have had that drug overdose!" I turned and ran away, away from that church, from all those people judging me for what I'd done. Got a job on the island, packed up my stuff and left.

3pm. Five hours to go

Bloody hell. I'm even more unfit than I thought. I struggle to the highest point of the track and collapse in a heap on the damp, leafy ground. I can make out the quarry in the distance, enough to see that there are people there but not what they're doing. I cough, a rattling smoker's hack. It's worryingly bad, since I only started smoking when I was at university – not even ten years ago.

For the first time, I doubt if my escape plan will work. Will I even have the physical strength to do it?

Na na na na-na-na-naa…

I get up and keep walking. I must get to our spot. That much I owe Dan, owe us, before my time is up. I have to say goodbye to the old him the only way I know how.

When I first met Dan, he drove me to the quarry. He explained that the water was very deep in most places, but in this spot there were rocks that would dash you to pieces. It became our place.

We spent long hours there under the cover of the thick trees, talking, smoking weed and having sex. Even after the noise started, I could never hear it from that spot, for some reason.

It was there I told Dan about Morgan, in the early days of our relationship. He's still the only person here I've told what happened.

"Babe, it wasn't your fault," he said, stroking my hair, which had grown long and straight since moving to the island.

"I could've done more." My hands picked up the dry, brown leaves from the ground and crushed them to tiny fragments as I talked, avoiding Dan's gaze.

He put his hand under my chin and turned my face towards him. "Listen to me. We all have regrets. We all blame ourselves. But you looked after her for so long. There is only so much you can do to help people who are self-destructive."

"Everyone blames me. Our friends, our parents."

He shook his head. "Then where were they? Did they help? Why do they think you were the only one who should've done something?"

I buried my head into Dan's chest and wept. "She comes to me, at night. Always."

He put his arms around me and held me tight until I finished crying. For the first time, the pain and guilt of losing Morgan receded slightly, and I felt everything would be alright as long as Dan was here.

Na na na na-na-na-naa…

I wish that Dan was here.

For another twenty minutes, I force my burning thighs and

heaving lungs along. I stop just before the quarry, sit on a stone and light a cigarette. A single bird flies in a circle overhead, singing. It's a lorikeet, maybe, or a galah, although I'm still terrible at identifying the bird species here. I can hear voices – the investigators, no doubt. I hope they can't hear me. They would be way too interested in me being here. They've probably been talking about me already.

The noise starts again, Jane, Jane, Jane, and this time Morgan's voice is sickly sweet, coaxing.

I stand up and push myself along the path that goes around the quarry. Na na na na-na-na-naa. I huff and puff until I get to the two entwined trees which signals it's time to turn right. Five minutes later, another few twists and turns around and past the old Stoneco site office, and I'm at our spot. Disturbances in the gravel near the edge make it look like someone's been here recently, but that can't be true – no one except Dan and I know to come here.

The water, as ever, is hypnotically flat, and a sparkling shade of aqua blue, contrasting starkly with the white limestone, which is blinding in the high summer sun. As always, I'm taken aback by the beauty of this place. Beats the muddy old Thames, anyway.

The quarry is unusually full of people. Some are setting up tents by the road, and some are down near the water, but I can't make out what they're doing. How frustrating. I used to have 20/20 vision but my eyesight seems to have gotten a lot worse recently. Perhaps I should get glasses?

I walk over to the edge and look straight into the water. It's a long way down. I stare so hard I begin to feel dizzy, and the blue green water bounces towards me, then away. I imagine myself falling, down, down into that blue. My feet shuffle closer and closer to the edge and suddenly, my right foot slips on the rubble and slides towards the quarry below. For a moment, I think it's all over.

Then, I manage to get control of my leg, take a large step back and collapse on my bottom. My right knee pops. That will be painful later. My breath comes fast. Still, I pull myself up and charge away – away from our place, from everything that happened here. Away from the eyes of all those people, who probably saw the rocks falling and now know our secret spot.

Na na na na-na-na-naa...

Once I'm back on the main track, the noise starts again, but this time it's not Morgan calling my name. It's Dan. Jane, Jane, Jane. His voice is loving and fun, the voice of the man I fell in love with. Old Dan.

5pm. Three hours to go

At first, I keep running down the track, then into the bush without much thought for where I'm going, ignoring my screaming lungs, my throbbing thighs, my aching right knee. I try to use the pain to push Dan's voice out of my head, stop it saying Jane, Jane, Jane. His tone is teasing now, sarcastic.

Na na na...

It's only once I'm on the Quarry Road near the camping grounds, well clear of the quarry, and turn north-east that I realise I'm heading towards Amama Harbour. The Quarry Road is wide and well-built, as it was once the main route for taking the limestone from the quarry down to the harbour.

That's it, I can finally do something productive, rather than just killing time waiting – I can go and scope out the harbour, work out which boat to steal. All I need is something small with an outboard motor. Then, I can row for a bit under the cover of darkness, until I'm far enough to start the motor without anyone hearing. I'll be back on the mainland well before dawn, and in a city before anyone realises I'm gone.

6pm. Two hours to go

Amama Harbour is a long, hot walk. A dusty, unshaded, trip through hell, with Dan's voice echoing from the quarry now behind me. A blister is forming on the back of my left heel, where it's been rubbing against my old canvas shoe. I wish I'd thought to bring water.

Na na na na-na-na-naa…

When I'm almost at the harbour, I realise how stupid I've been. It's a dangerous place for someone like me to go. Going there will certainly raise suspicion. Everyone's always watching me in this place, especially down at the harbour.

I pause for a minute, wondering what to do, torn between my desire to plan my escape and perhaps find out what's happening with the investigation, and my fear.

No, it's safer to go home. Dan always avoids the harbour, says it's the only way not to be the topic of town gossip.

I turn off the road and onto a rough bike trail that will take me towards home. The trail's covered with a thick canopy of trees and my burning face welcomes the relief from the sun. I'm lucky I haven't bumped into anyone yet. It was stupid to go out, when I'm so close to escape.

7pm. One hour to go

I'm back home. I'll stay here until it gets dark. My eyes shut and I lean back on the sofa, body exhausted, my mind too wired to shut down. Dan's still in my thoughts. I imagine him lying on the ground next to me, looking up at the trees, holding my hand and laughing.

Na na na na-na-na-naa…

Then the noise sounds again and this time Dan's voice is sad and angry, and I have the image of the last time I saw him, at our spot at the quarry, face pinched and pale with anger.

I shiver at the memory, with renewed terror that they'll find Dan's body – at the bottom of the quarry, where it's been for the past two weeks. My last secret. Funny how I keep referring to him as if he's still alive. Habit, I suppose.

On the night it happened, Dan drove me out to our spot. We sat on a rock a couple of metres from the edge, but he didn't put his arm around me like normal. I lit a joint, but when I went to pass it to him, he shook his head.

"I've decided to return to the mainland." His words were so sudden my brain took a few seconds to digest the information.

"Okay, I'm happy to leave the island if that's what you want."

"No. You see, I need you to stay. I mean, I need to go alone." He looked at me sideways, running a hand through his blonde hair.

"So you're breaking up with me?" I tried to take his arm but he pulled away with a jerk.

"Yes, Jane, I am. I'm sorry."

"But why? I thought you loved me." I tried again to touch him, but this time he stood up and moved away from me.

"Because we're terrible for each other. We drag each other down and we'll end up stuck in misery forever."

I stood to move closer to him again. "How can you say that? We understand each other."

He stepped back, his once-loving eyes so hard and cold that I felt a stabbing in my heart. "Probably too well. This depression, this self-pity you're stuck in since your sister died – you have to let it go. You're making yourself ill, Jane, have been since I met you."

"You're one to talk, mate. You had a breakdown because you couldn't take the pressure of a stupid job!"

His eyebrows lowered and he waved his finger at me, as if he were the school teacher. "I know Jane, but unlike you, I want to get better. All you want to do is wallow in the past."

We'd moved nearer to the edge, so close I could see the reflection of the moon in the water. "My sister died and you want me to get over it?"

"I do, yes. But I know now you never will and I can't stay here with you. I need to get away, start again, try and be happy."

I wanted him to stop, unable to believe what I was hearing. "You said you would always be there for me."

"I can't, Jane. I thought I could, but I just can't."

I lunged at him, the anger, the betrayal, flying out of my fists and beating him on the chest, the stomach, the groin. "I trusted you! I told you about Morgan!"

He stepped back again, to get away from me. And suddenly he was gone, over the edge and onto the sharp rocks below.

Na na na na-na-na-naa…

There was a time when I was a good person, I was, really, when I would've gone straight to the police and told them the truth, said that Dan and I had gotten into a fight and he'd fallen into the quarry. But if even my own parents blamed me for what happened to Morgan, how could I expect anyone to believe I didn't mean to kill Dan?

So instead I made my way to the harbour. First, I found Dan's boat and filled it with big stones, then pushed it out into the water and drilled holes in the bottom until it sank. It was a long swim back to shore but in my focused state I swam slowly and surely.

Everyone knows everyone else's business on this island, but I learned how to turn the power of gossip to my advantage. All I had to do was whisper that someone had seen him leaving early for the mainland and it was carved in stone three hours later. It raised no suspicion – they all hated me so probably thought Dan was doing well to leave me.

I didn't know exactly how Dan's dad had gotten the money to send him to school. But I knew where that money was kept. Oh, yes. We'd worked it out, old Dan and I, broke the code that his dad had left behind, found the spot where he'd buried the money on their property, far away from banks and tax people and anyone else who might be unnecessarily nosy about where it'd come from – Dan promised me that we'd use that money to buy a lovely house on the mainland and be happy. Well, before things changed.

Na na na na-na-na-naa…

After Dan fell off the edge of the quarry, my plan was to leave a few weeks later, to avoid suspicion. I took pains to keep the lie going.

Dan was hopelessly predictable with his computer passwords, so I emailed a few people to say how he'd left this 'awful island' and 'crazy girlfriend' at last. It almost worked too well, and I had to resist the temptation to argue with the people who agreed with what a good move he'd made.

It was all going so smoothly... until today. Until they started investigating that bloody noise.

Just one hour to go. One hour until it gets dark and I can escape safely. Dig up the money and run away into the darkness, start again.

Na na na na-na-na-naa...

7.45pm. 15 minutes to go

There's a knock. My heart stops. I open the door and see a man and woman standing under umbrellas. They aren't in uniform but by their manner I guess they're coppers. And not the local officers, Hartono and Mully, but mainlanders. It's raining. A soft drizzle.

"What can I do for you?"

"We'd just like to have a word, Miss..."

"Langfield." I lean against the peeling door frame, trying not to sound either too nervous or too casual. *You're so close to escape, just stay cool.* "Sure, come in."

"No, that's alright. We won't be long. We're just investigating the noise coming from the quarry. Sorry to disturb you, but we are trying to interview everyone who lives on the island, or everyone who was born here and now lives on the mainland. You're one of the few people we haven't spoken to, so we're just wondering what you know about the noise?"

My stomach tightens. Well, Officer, the noise is the ghost of my sister, for whose death I'm responsible. But don't investigate it any further, please, as I'd rather you didn't discover the body of my boyfriend, in whose death I also played a part. Oh, and *Hey Jude* has been stuck in my head for a very long time. Any idea how I can get it out? "Nothing much. I hear it from time to time. Obviously, as I live quite close to the quarry."

"Do you have any idea what it means?"

"Just sounds like a moan to me."

The woman cop, who's about thirty, with short curly dark hair, squeezes her lips together. "Yes... that's what almost everyone says."

I know she's hinting she thinks there's more but I don't want to go down that route. I'm not telling her about Morgan and Dan. "Are you... dredging?"

She looks at me closely. "There are many parts to our investigation, but I'm afraid I can't discuss them with you."

I try to talk, but only a stammer comes out. The man, who's older, in his fifties maybe, gives me a very strange look.

"Of course, it would be better if my boyfriend – ex-boyfriend – Dan were here. He knows more about this island than me, far more."

"That's okay," says the woman. "We spoke to Dan on the mainland just a few days ago. He was most helpful."

"You saw Dan?"

"Yes. Short blonde fella. Bit of a beer belly."

On impulse, I run inside and grab a picture of Dan and I, taken when we first met, then come back out and thrust it in their faces.

Na na na na-na-na-naa...

"Yeah, him," says the woman. Her voice is kind, too kind. "We went to his home on the mainland. Except, he hasn't got as much hair as in this picture and he's older, of course."

"Older? But this was taken a few months ago."

The man steps in. "Miss, he's been living on the mainland for fifteen years. He mentioned you were once in a relationship and he lets you live here in his house. I don't know what his wife thinks about that, but it's none of my business of course."

"But that's... impossible. We only just broke up – we got together last year when I moved here."

The two cops look at each other, and I see their expressions changing. Pity.

The woman takes my hand quietly and I look down at it, seeing lines where there were none before – the hands of a woman who's over forty, not the smooth skin of a woman not yet thirty. I remember how difficult it was for me to get to the top of the peak. Was it just unfitness, an early smokers' cough?

I step away from them. Then I look down further and see my thighs – they are seriously large. So is my belly. The body of an obese woman. When did I gain all this weight? My long hair falls around me; mousy brown, heavily streaked with grey.

Hey Jude continues to play in my head, louder and louder and I can hear the noise too, shouting "Jane, Jane, Jane, Jane." Dan, Morgan, Jane – they're all just names, just tricks.

The cops thank me and get away as fast as they can.

As soon as they're out of sight, I grab my trowel, torch, a large sack from the shed, and run into the garden. Dark will fall soon, so I dig frantically, down into the dirt between the roots of a large tree, digging, digging in the spot where the box with the money is buried. Nothing. It's gone. The money's all gone. I look up at the rainclouds, thin but insistent. It's so hot still, like a storm's brewing. If it comes, there'll be no escaping the island tonight.

I collapse into a heap next to the hole, leaning against the tree trunk and pulling the sack over my head. I close my eyes to think things through, and find myself drift towards a doze. I don't know how much later it is, but when I hear a rustle nearby I peek out from under the sack. Through the semi-darkness, I see a barefoot young man coming towards me, wearing a torn, damp t-shirt. I recognise him – that deaf kid, Harold. I pull the sack back over my head, hoping he hasn't seen me.

I hear him walk up to me and then stand still. A moment later, the noise says my name again: Jane, Jane, Jane. Except this time, it sounds like my own voice: Jane, Jane, Jane.

A familiar guitar melody fills the air and I realise Harold's playing a song. It takes me until the chorus to recognise it as *Hotel California*. The smooth voice moves into the corners of my brain, finally pushing out *Hey Jude*. The lyrics tell me what I have known all along.

I can never leave...

Alex Cain is a writer and journalist who makes a living penning stories on everything from pharmaceuticals to planes. She is also working on The House with Eleven Windows, a series of historical fiction novels set in Finland and Russia.

Sometimes caring leads to misperceptions...

The Big Dipper

Sonia Zadro

Rosie

Harry wasn't keen to meet up tonight with all the coppas around investigating 'the noise' at the quarry. What a farce. I tell you something hasn't made me laugh so hard since little Perry farted at the start of his dance recital in front of the whole bloody town. People have been whinging about this noise for bonkers; old Marlene down at the camping ground, Alice and Joey at the community centre, Neves and Elaine and all the rest of the oldies, not to mention the crowd who live near new Jane's school cabin. They're acting like a bunch of spooked new agers if you ask me. I ain't never heard any noise around here, so either I'm deaf or this town's crazy, and I'm not deaf. Okay, the ears are a tad rusty but the other oldies like Shirley Hanley and Nannette Darcy have kept me sane, and I've never been one for spooks or ghosts, or murder mysteries. What you see is what you get, and if you're seeing something like spooks or ghosts then that's just your imagination wanting you to believe that the world is a whole lot more interesting than it really is.

Unless it's love. Corny as hell I know, but I can feel it. I can feel it and I can see it written all over Harry's face whenever I surprise him at his bedroom window for our secret nightly rendezvous. His rugged old looks light right up like Cecile Marbo's front porch at Christmas. It warms my heart just thinking about Harry's face when he looks at me. We usually go to a private spot no one knows of, we secretly named Huon's Nest. It's a small cave facing the ocean and it dazzles me every time. It's on the south side of the island at least seven kilometres from anyone, and you can only get to it through a low valley of Huon pines which stretch up to a high cliff face – one of the highest spots on all the island, overlooking a small beach. Harry and I take an unused road, a mile past the quarry, and drive up to where the stretch of pines begins, hiding our car in a clearing between two of them. Then we hop out and manoeuvre around a bunch of boulders right along the cliff's edge to reach the cave, which looks out over a vast dark ocean. A moon sometimes trails its milky ink right on up to where we lie, thick and heavy, a bright diamond weight.

You're probably thinking I'm quite a poet for an old bird – but I've always had the poetic streak deep down. Just thinking about Harry and Huon's Nest brings it right out of me. Add a beautiful moonlit night and you won't shut me up, I'll just keep carrying on and on about the moon forever. And Harry loves it when I speak all romantic – it makes him want to ravish me all over. So I slip in the odd phrase whenever I can.

Harry always brings a rug, and a gas lamp on our rendezvous, in case the moon isn't out or hidden behind thick clouds, as they often are here on the island. Once there, we always stay real quiet for a while, just stunned by the vastness of the black deep before us, and the flooded canopy of bright stars arching overhead. Give me a night like that any night of the year and I'll be the happiest woman alive. A night like that – then pair it with the Big Dipper – and you'll never take the smile off my face.

After the quiet, I never give Harry the chance to talk. We just get straight in there and are all over each other like old Marlene's foot rash. Though it's a whole lot more passionate and beautiful than how that sounds. And it always ends with me going so high I'm sure I'm right up there with the stars.

After a lot of arguing, I finally persuaded Harry to meet up tonight, but he wanted to try Blackwood Forest. I'm not keen, though, on mucking about in the dark of the forest. More chance of ticks and redbacks, and red-belly blacks amongst the trees. Not romantic as far as I'm concerned.

So I told him I just wanted to go to Huon's Nest on our rug with the sea spread out wide and huge before us and the moon hanging like an angel's lantern lighting up our love. There was no way I was letting Harry do his Big Dipper in Blackwood Forest, no way. One, I would be too terrified of the crawlies finding their way to my naked body; and two, Cecile Marbo who I played Trivia with on Monday nights, lived only a quarter mile away from Blackwood Forest, and with the way she'd taken to wandering lately it would just be my luck to have her spring us both while Harry was smack bang in the middle of his dipper. Quite frankly I couldn't think of anything more off-putting.

Right on nine, as planned, I was outside Harry's window and he slipped out and into the driver's seat of his pick-up truck so fast and so silent we were like a pair of pros. He wasn't a big talker, Harry, but his face was all lit up again with excitement, and the odd look across at me while he changed gears. I was wearing my old sleeveless pink nightie covered in tiny white roses and had given my hair a purple silver rinse only yesterday – the one Harry said highlighted the blue in my eyes. The weather was warm and slick, just how I like it. It had also started to rain and a storm was brewing. Some would have been put right off by this but I loved a good storm. Anything to make things more wild and romantic is always a goer, I say. But Harry took a left towards Blackwood, away from the usual right that headed way south down towards Huon's Nest.

"Not this again – I'm not doing it in Blackwood, Harry, not with all those creepy crawlies, and there's no way in this storm."

He glanced across and frowned. "Too many coppas towards Huon's Nest, sweet. It runs right alongside the quarry. A lone pick-up truck out in the dark during the investigation, they'll stop us for sure. Then Rhonda will find out, with Mully on the case."

Officer Mully was the biggest source of gossip Amama Harbour had. You'd think a coppa was more professional but not in this isolated place. He operated the night shift, back to back with Officer Hartono, and he craved drama. Rhonda was Harry's wife and before you think my Harry's a cheating, lying bastard let me explain that Rhonda has been in half the pants of all the men now over seventy on this island, beginning the day after they were married back in 1945. Used him for his money she did, and kept him under her nasty ass-whipping thumb, with her yelling and shoving since the day they wed. Refused a divorce too. 'It's not respectable for a respectable woman,' she would say. That always made me laugh harder than anything, her saying she was respectable.

I had to insist to Harry about Blackwood. There's no way I was going there. "If they stop us, I'll just say we were really excited by the investigation and wanted to check it out."

Harry rolled his eyes at me.

"It's the first time we've ever had more than two police officers on the island. Why wouldn't they buy it?" I insisted.

"Because Mully suspects something's fishy already. Rhonda and I were at West White Beach when you were swimming there Saturday morning. He caught me staring at you in the water. Told me to be patient and wait till I got home with Rhonda. Then he laughed like a bloody banshee. No doubt spread it around town as well – what a horny old bastard I am."

I turned and trailed my fingers along Harry's arm. "Yeah? Well I'm glad you're a horny old bastard. You were staring at me in the water? I'll bet he laughed."

"It's not like it's that surprising." Harry gave me one of his sexy dark looks. "Everyone knows you're the hottest thing on the island."

He grinned. "Everyone over seventy that is. And if Blackwood's too far out, sweet, how about the trees behind Jimmy's scuba shop?"

I gently squeezed his arm. "Take me to Huon tonight, Harry. You show me The Big Dipper in front of that fat moon spilling its light right up to where we are lying together and I promise, you won't even think about your age for a second. I'll deal with Mully. Promise."

Harry smiled, "That's if the moon lasts in this weather, love."

Officer Johnson

I left my gun on the mainland by accident and I've never regretted anything so much in my life. At night this quarry's especially eerie; big, vast, hollow, black, and so quiet. Like waiting for someone or something to emerge, anything to break that emptiness and blackness. But when the silence did break it was terrifying – this dissonant repetitive wail, an echo of pain, almost like a scream, yet muffled so you couldn't quite make it out. Was it a human voice? Was it in pain? Perhaps there were several voices? Maybe it wasn't a voice at all but an old large bit of pipe lost somewhere and catching the wind? Thank goodness this assignment was expected to last only a day. I don't mind the occasional murder case but I'm terrified of ghosts and all things supernatural. I'm also new to the force, at the tail end of my training and currently completing an internship. A female officer in training, admitting they are terrified of ghosts – not something I want on my record. Especially when I'm trying to prove my capabilities to the other male officers. I could just see it: *Was the officer able to cope with stressful situations while on duty? FAIL.* I was determined to keep my fear of all things spooky very quiet.

The noise started up again as the rain started falling heavier. I could see we were in for a storm so I was glad that myself and the other officers searching with me, had been ordered to stick to some caves just south of the quarry. Someone thought there might be a hidden natural watercourse connecting the caves to the quarry.

We'd finished searching two of them, which extended northward for a kilometre along the south coast of the island and the noise seemed to get quieter so we turned back and made our way along a more extensive series of caves which ran southwards. Having been called onto the island, we'd never been through these caves, so Officer Mully joined us.

After an hour walking south the noise became louder, then abruptly stopped. Ten minutes later it started up again, and the further south we went the louder it became. Not only was it louder, and clearly audible through the rain, but to me it definitely sounded human, possibly animal. But this was no windy pipe.

My palms began to sweat. Creepies crawled all over me. The noise seemed to increase and echo all around the cave we were in, making blood rapidly drain from my head and into my feet. Along with the confines of this stuffy enclosed darkness, it was too much for me, for too long, and I started feeling dizzy and faint. If my heart raced any faster I was sure I'd pass out.

We stepped into a large cave about fifty meters wide and I could hear the faint sound of the ocean getting closer. We must have been at the southern end of the island after walking for over two hours. I couldn't take it anymore so I sat down.

"Johnson, everything okay?" Mully asked.

"Sure." I gulped air down in slow steady breaths. "Sorry, sir. I'm just not great in confined spaces."

A torch flash on my face, which I knew would have been covered in sweat and looking pale as ash. "How about you wait here and catch your breath, Johnson. Given the sound of those waves, these caves must end a hundred odd metres down that tunnel there."

Relief weighed me down and I couldn't even speak. I just nodded and put my head down between my legs to get the blood back into it. It was creepy here – but not as creepy as the thought of what that noise could be, and it was getting louder and louder by the minute.

Mully kept talking to me while my brain filled back up with

blood. "You look like you need some fresh air. We'll all take a break. When you catch your breath, you head on up ahead through the tunnel and grab some air at the end."

My eyes flew open. Grab some air? Up there at the end of the tunnel? In the direction of that terrifying noise? Was he crazy?

I felt my head spin all over again so I stayed like that with my head down for quite some time. I couldn't tell Mully I was terrified of ghosts or whatever that sound was. He'd report back to my boss on the mainland and I might not pass as fit to serve in the force. Then there'd be the endless wisecracks from the other officers. I forced down my terror and raised my head.

"I'm ready now," I croaked. "I'll go and get some air."

Mully shone the torch at me and frowned. "I won't be far behind you, Johnson."

I grabbed my torch and forced myself to focus.

Once out of sight of the officers and around the bend of the tunnel, I stamped my feet trying to get more blood into them and shook my head to clear it. That was when the echoes through the tunnel got louder. I nearly dropped my torch, but if I didn't get to the end, now, I'd never get there.

I forced myself forward and saw the opening ahead. The smell of salt from the sea was getting stronger so I sucked in the clean air. All the while the sound kept getting clearer through the downpour of rain, like a wild piercing scream echoing through the caves. I decided to make a run for it to the opening, my head pounding and spinning. I was so dizzy my vision began to blur.

At the end, my heart stopped as I stood staring, terrified at what I could see in the darkness. A ten-limbed monster roared at the top of its lungs. Lightning flashed and I glimpsed a mop of silvery purple hair amid many limbs. I heard a scream, realised it was me screaming, then turned and ran straight back into Mully, tripping over in the process.

"Good God, Johnson, what on earth is it?"

"A m… m… monster," I sputtered. I could barely speak so I just shook my head, grateful the sound had stopped.

Mully withdrew his gun. "I'm going out there. Don't you worry, Johnson."

The other officers had caught up to Mully now and were right behind him, guns drawn. When they turned the corner, I waited for their screams. Instead I heard Mully's voice.

"Rosie? Harry? Is that you?"

Suddenly I heard Mully grunting, and shouting. "Hey, lay off, you crazy woman!"

A woman began screaming at him, hysterically. Was the woman being attacked by the monster?

To my surprise, several of the officers started laughing. It was muffled at first and then became louder. I peered around the corner and saw an older man sitting naked with a pair of shorts covering his lap and an older woman – wrapped in a blanket and nothing else – vigorously attacking Officer Mully with a thermos flask.

"You dirty bastards!" She was wild. "How do you expect Harry and me to come back now? To our nest! To our dipper! You pervs have ruined everything!" Her mop of silver purple hair was flying everywhere.

Silver purple hair?

I shook my head and couldn't believe it. It all took a few moments to sink in, for my adrenalin to settle down, for me to realise my mistake.

I covered my mouth with my hand and stifled a laugh. I was never going to live this down after all.

Soon after, walking back through the caves, I was still smiling at my own stupidity. I lingered some way behind the other officers, not caring about the darkness or confined space. If what I'd just been through couldn't cure my fear of ghosts nothing would.

Then, from way behind I heard a sound. A frightening, dissonant repetitive sound.

And it was no windy pipe.

Sonia Zadro is a freelance writer of feature articles for magazines such as Wellbeing Australia and Nature and Health. Her first short story, Oscar, received a highly commended in the BezerkaCon 2016 Short Story competition for speculative fiction and her work as a clinical psychologist provides inspiration for her characters and their struggles. She is currently working on a novel and several short stories.

Sometimes caring takes a lot from us...

Chasing Rabbit Holes

A.R Kelly

"This is so typical of you to blame me, Archie. Do you think I planned on losing it?" I stood over my fiancé as he crawled on the floor on his hands and knees, running his fingers over every inch of bare surface. The cabin had already been tipped upside down. He'd pulled clothes out of bags, and sifted through all our belongings in the hunt for the missing ring. Even the mattress didn't escape his scrutiny, and it was now lying exposed in the middle of the bedroom, sheets thrown in a heap on the floor, waiting for me to pick them up.

"That ring belonged to my grandmother," Archie said. "It was a family heirloom, Sarah. I gave it you to keep forever and you lost it in less than four months." He crawled into the kitchen like a giant, angry baby, wailing insults as the pearlescent shells that screened the doorway fluttered and clicked in his wake.

I clenched my jaw to stop myself from telling him what I really thought. As usual, he had gone and done something without thinking it through, and I was getting the blame for it going wrong. "This wouldn't have happened if you hadn't brought me out here into the middle of nowhere." I followed him into the kitchen. "If we had gone on a real holiday instead, like a normal couple."

He looked up from rifling through the garbage bin. "This is better than a holiday, Sarah. It's an adventure – and where else would you rather be?" He went back to sifting through garbage, ignoring my eye-roll. "We have to find it. My mother always said it's bad luck for women to take their wedding ring off."

"Your mother says a lot of things which don't mean much."

"What was that?"

"Nothing." I pulled out a dining chair, scraping it across the scarred kitchen floor before plonking myself in front of him. The plume of three-day old baked fish slowly spread across the kitchen. "I'm sure it'll turn up Arch. We've only been at the beach or community centre."

He pulled out bits of rubbish and studied each item before tossing them into a plastic shopping bag.

"And I always left my jewellery here when we went to beach because I didn't want to lose anything. So it must be at the community centre. Or maybe the local store. Let's ask around to see if anyone has seen it. I'll put some signs up offering a reward."

I did feel bad about his grandmother's ring, but was also glad to be rid of the garish thing – a chunky, yellow gold band topped with an ostentatious latticework of multi-coloured stones. Despite knowing that it wasn't to my taste Archie had, as usual, expected me to go along with his 'family tradition'. He also knew how exhausted I was from the lack of sleep because of the nightly noise and light show, but that was *my* problem as far as he was concerned.

Every single night, like clockwork, the noise would start up accompanied by the purple glow that no-one else seemed to notice but me. Covering up the windows didn't make any difference as I could still feel its glow on me, even when I closed my eyes. It was driving me mad, and what made it worse was that every time I tried to talk to the locals about the light, they pretended they didn't know what I was talking about. The only person who seemed to pay any attention to it was Jack, which didn't fill me with much comfort given that Jack was also the local drunk.

Archie pulled his hands out of the bin and stood, stretching his back. "What about the quarry?"

"What?" His words cut through the fog sifting around my brain.

"The quarry. Let's go have another look up there today. You could have lost it when we had that picnic."

He walked over to the kitchen sink and washed his hands. "Ow! They need to fix this tap, it's either freezing or peels your skin off." He winced, hands hovering over the sink. "Remind me when we give the keys back."

"No," I said, ignoring his comment about the water. "No way am I going back up there." I was already shaking my head. "I told you, that quarry gives me the creeps." I wrapped my arms tightly across my chest. "There's no way I'm going there again."

"What if it's up there? We need to search before someone else finds it."

"Who? One of the other non-existent tourists? No one else goes up there. The locals stay away from the place, and the only ones stupid enough to go up there are visitors like us who then end up being tormented by the noise." I stood, pushing the chair back. "Jack said the quarry has something to do with the noise, and it's where I always see the purple light. If you want to go, then go right ahead."

The shiny shells jumped and rattled as I flung them aside on my way out.

Daylight was fading fast as I stepped outside to clear my head. A walk was what I needed. I shoved my hands in the pockets of my rain jacket and realised I'd left my phone behind, but decided to not go back for it. Thick black clouds raced overhead, bringing the first rumbles of thunder over the sea. It had threatened to storm all day, so Archie had elected not to come, and I was relieved to have some time to myself. The palm trees fringing our cabin tossed around in the approaching winds, and I pulled my jacket tight to buffer against them. It was too early for the bar, so I ducked into the local store to grab a snack.

The shopkeeper Roj was serving some people I hadn't seen before – a woman and man who looked like they were dressed head to toe in brand new clothes, large dark glasses covering half their faces. The only other person in the store was that strange deaf kid, a local who just stared and smiled at people.

The couple walked out and got into a blue car that also looked new, then drove off up Cove Road. I hung back in the freezer aisle until they were gone before stepping up to the counter.

Roj gave me a grin that slowly bloomed out from around his mouth to fill his entire face with smile lines. It was hard to feel glum around Roj. "Sarah! Haven't seen you around for a few days. How are you enjoying your holiday?"

"Well enough, Roj." I smiled back. "I'm looking forward to going back home though. Looking forward to sleeping in my own bed."

He took my ice cream and swiped it over the register. "Hm, I know what you mean." He nodded as I dropped some coins into his palm.

"Roj who were those people just now? Are they tourists? The mainland boat won't be here for a few days yet, so I was wondering how they got here."

"They probably came over in the helicopter." He seemed to be telling himself as much as he was me. "I don't remember hearing one though, did you?"

"All I ever hear is that brain-melting noise; all I ever see are those bright lights in the quarry." I puffed out a sigh as I watched his face, not missing how he kept his eyes down and busied himself with the register.

"Yes, the ocean has been loud these past few nights." He spoke without looking up. "And the moon particularly bright. It's usually a sign of bad weather on its way." He gave me another wide smile, handing over my change. This time his smile looked embarrassed.

———

I headed over to the community centre with my ice cream, hoping to bump into the new arrivals again. By now, the noise had begun its familiar thumping inside my head. Jack was sitting at the bar in his usual spot, his tattered khaki t-shirt looking even more crumpled and beer-stained than usual.

He was the only local who believed me when I mentioned both noise and light. He'd said other tourists had been driven away by the noise, but he hadn't heard about the light before I mentioned it. Joey, the young bar manager, usually laughed him off when she overheard us, telling me that Jack spent more time in the bar than he did at home and not to listen to him. It was sad to admit, but right now it felt like he was my only friend on the island.

"So we haven't scared you off yet, eh?" He turned to greet me.

"No, but I'll be glad to get off this miserable rock," I threw back as I pulled out the bar stool next to him. I inched in as close as I could without wrinkling my nose at the smell of stale beer rolling off him. "I saw some new arrivals in Roj's store just now, but the boat isn't due for days. And I didn't hear a helicopter, did you?"

He stared into his drink, not answering.

"Jack?"

"Scientists. Mully and OHar organised them. I try and stay out of it." He tipped his glass back and took a long drink before going back to staring into the beer.

"Stay out of what, Jack? How did they get here if there's no boat and if there wasn't any helicopter?"

"Just because we didn't hear a helicopter doesn't mean there wasn't one here. But," he took a deep breath and slumped his shoulders, flicking his eyes around the bar before continuing, "there is another way onto the island," he mumbled.

I folded my arms on the bar table and leaned closer to him.

"Through the quarry? There's something going on in that place, isn't there?"

Jack pressed his cracked lips together and gave a small nod.

"Archie wants to go back to there tonight. I've lost my engagement ring and he thinks I might have dropped it there." I watched his face.

His hand trembled as he pulled his drink to his mouth.

"I don't want to to go of course – not since I'm the only one who seems to see the purple light."

Jack coughed into his beer. "Don't talk about that here." He glanced around again. "You haven't told anyone else that you can see that light, have you?"

"No. Other than Archie, you're the only other person I've told."

"Good." He furrowed his brows as he looked at me. "It's better for you to not speak about that to anyone. And stay away from the quarry, it's not a good place."

"I wish you would tell Archie. He doesn't seem to think there's anything strange about that place at all. I don't want to go anywhere near that place again."

The first few drops of rain were starting to fall as I got back to the cabin. The thick clouds were blotting out the last remaining light of the day. I pushed the door open, sliding my hand over the wall to flick on a light. Archie wasn't there, and I already guessed where he'd gone before reading the messages waiting on my phone:

Need help. Can you come get me? Please hurry. On road.

Above this was an earlier message:

Gone to the quarry to find the ring.

Dread gnawed at the base of my stomach as I read the messages again. "Of all the nights," I said aloud into the empty cabin. He could have waited till morning, at least that wouldn't have been as bad as having to go up there in a raging storm.

I pushed my phone into the back pocket of my jeans and stepped outside again. The hood of my jacket flapped against my face as I jogged back into town in the rain. The storm was almost overhead now, and the rain howled off the sea in a horizontal sheet, turning Cove Road into a huge wind tunnel.

I cut across to the police station. It was locked. "Officer Mully?" I banged on the door. "OHar, are you there?"

No answer.

Jack had said they'd organised the scientists. Perhaps they were with them?

Alice, the nurse from the community centre, she might have a radio. All tourists were told where she lived on their arrival.

I hurried back toward the local store. Alice's house was two doors down from there. But the road had turned into a stream, and my feet squelched beneath me as I battled against the downpour.

"Alice!" I thumped my palm on her door. "Alice!"

The door swung open after a few more bangs, and the island's only medical expert peeked out into the storm.

"Alice, I'm Sarah, we met last night at Trivia? I'm sorry to come to you like this, but my partner needs help and I can't find Mully or OHar."

"Oh you poor thing. Come in." Alice stepped aside.

I stepped through the door, and onto a large sheltered verandah. A pool of water darkened the polished wood beneath my feet. "Sorry about the mess." I looked down at my soaked clothes.

"Oh don't worry about that," she laughed. "I've had to clean up much worse than a puddle of rain! Stay here a minute, I'll get you a towel."

"Thanks, but I'm only going to get wet again out there." The noise pierced my brain as I struggled to speak.

Alice turned back from the door leading into the house. "Don't worry, Sarah, we can drive to the quarry and get Archie in just a few minutes."

I stopped feeling bad about the puddle to look at her. I hadn't said anything about the quarry. "Thanks, Alice. That's... very kind of you."

"Of course dear, it's my job to care." She walked into another part of the house. "Let me try and get a hold of OHar." She came back in with a small bundle. "Here, I've got you some dry clothes. These are OHar's but I'm sure she won't mind you borrowing them." She handed me a black t-shirt and pair of jeans I might have fit into if I were still ten years old.

"Thank you Alice, but I have to find Archie. Please, he might be hurt."

"Of course. I'll get my bag." Alice smiled at me as she walked back into the house.

Through the front door was a lounge area, and on the coffee table in the middle of the room sat a bunch of keys. *Bingo.* I stepped inside and slid the keys off the table, tucking them into my pocket just as Alice walked back into the room.

She glanced at the table with a small frown. "That's funny, I thought I left my keys there. Let me check the bedside table."

I bolted as soon as she turned her back, leaving the front door open as I ran out. Thankfully her car was parked at the front, and beeped to life as I pressed the starter key.

The noise was screaming inside my head now, louder than ever. I drove as fast I could up Cove Road with next to zero visibility. There was a light flashing in my rearview mirror but there was no time to worry about whether Alice was following me as I sped up the hill.

Once I cleared the town, I slowed the stolen car to a crawl to look out for Archie, driving until the road finished near the base of the quarry. I was about to turn around and go back to search again when I noticed lights up ahead – not just the purple glow that normally accompanied the noise, but also what looked like headlights from another car.

I killed the lights and rolled to a stop near the line of trees that ran along the road behind the quarry's lake. The noise was hammering inside my head like the mother of all migraines.

The quarry was even more imposing at night, its huge black walls standing like silent sentinels against the backdrop of the lake, which roiled against the purple light. I had never seen the light up close before, and from up here it seemed to pulsate like a heartbeat in time with the noise. The air buzzed with an electric hum, and a metallic taste filled the inside of my mouth as I crept along the road, slowly nearing the lake.

The sky was dark now, and the light spilling out from the lake filled the quarry basin with a sickly purple glow. Silhouetted by the lake's edge, military tents billowed in the wind, flaps exposing equipment and devices to the rain. The only people visible were four figures standing on a track that lead to the top of the quarry, staring down at the water. The couple I saw at the store today were there, with two other men I didn't recognise. One was talking to the woman, while the other man had his back to me. Something about these strangers didn't feel right, so much that I had to fight the urge to run back into Amama Harbour. I had to find Archie, and these people might have seen him. I pulled myself up and walked over to them.

"You must be Sarah."

A woman in military uniform appeared out of nowhere, the nose of her gun pointed right between my eyes.

I threw my hands up in front of my face. "Please, I'm just looking for my fiancé." I struggled to hear myself speak against the mechanical whining inside my head.

"Then let's go find him." She nodded her gun towards the others and walked in pace behind me as we wound our way up the track.

The others didn't seem to notice that someone was holding a gun to my head.

"He's down there." The military woman gestured towards the lake. It was churning with huge spirals of purple light, which projected out in thin filaments and broke away like threads of fairy floss, blowing off into the trees.

The noise was making my bones tremble, like I was standing against a gigantic speaker. "Down there? Where? Where is he?" All I saw was light and sound.

"He's become the lake now." The woman from the store turned to look at me. Her eyes were shining with purple fire.

"Become the lake? You killed him?" I stared into the abyss. "Who are you people?"

The others turned to look at me with their purple eyes. One set of eyes was familiar. Archie stared through me like I wasn't there. The military woman loosened her grip and lifted her gun, nudging me towards the lake.

"We're the guardians of Helmuth Island, and we didn't kill him." She gave me a small smile as she pushed me forward. "We're saving him. We're saving you all."

"Helmuth Island?" I stumbled forward, trying to steady myself against the tide of noise and light rolling off the lake, drowning out my consciousness. "But that's not what this island's called." The magnetic energy of the lake pulled at me, and I could feel purple filaments seeping into my skin, wrapping around my mind, until I was completely enveloped by a beautiful prison of light. "Is it?"

"It's whatever you want it to be."

"How?" A tiny glint lit up the mud near my feet. I bent down and reached into the squelchy ooze. "Oh, I see." I pulled out the gold ring, and slipped it back on my finger. "I saw better than I ever had before." I smiled as I submitted to the lake. Yes, we would save everyone.

Azmeena Kelly is an environmental specialist and lawyer by day and spends her nights making up stories to validate the voices in her head. Writing mostly speculative fiction, Azmeena has published a number of short stories and flash fiction pieces, and is working on her first novel.

Sometimes what others want matters more...

The Nematode Worms

Malibu Bert

Daisy tied the heavy brown rope in a double hitch knot to secure her boat to the rusted cleat. She groaned with exertion, straining to pull the rope as tightly as she could, then squinted through the twilight to check it.

Her daughters, Karen and Jess, bobbed down on their haunches and also took turns to pull the rope.

"Yep," Daisy wheezed, pulling one last time after them. "We're not going to get that knot any tighter." She trailed her daughters who had already started up the jetty towards the main road. The wooden boards beneath them, once a freshly painted white, had splintered and frayed to a dirty grey, and they creaked in protest under the harried carriage of the trio as they headed towards the island's only town.

Large limestone rocks, worn by feet, tires and mining equipment from decades ago, popped up along the path doing double duty as crude cobblestones and trip hazards along an uneven path. They forced Daisy, Karen and Jess to pick their way carefully among them. Daisy thought she saw tiny red lines squiggling about in unison on the rocks, but rubbed her eyes and kept going. It was late and they'd been bobbing about on waves for too long – she was seeing things.

A low rumble of thunder rippled across the blackened sky, releasing heavy droplets of rain that splotched huge, wet patches onto the craggy, dry rocks. Daisy tipped her head back sharply, her brow furrowed, and scanned the blue-black clouds rolling in above them. "Oh my God! That's all we need." She grabbed Jess's hand, quickly glancing at her daughter's watch. "It's almost seven. Come on, girls. There's not a moment to lose."

She led her youngest daughter along the town's jagged, worn road, wondering again for the millionth time what had happened to her husband. How on Earth could he have taken off like that? And why had he lied to her? Anger and guilt swirled round and round in her head like a vicious cycle driving her mad.

"There was no warning, was there? With your father, I mean?" She squeezed Jess's hand firmly to demonstrate a reply was imperative.

"No, Mum. There was nothing," Jess reassured her again. "He ran off this morning without a word."

Another rumble of thunder felt like the heavens were also venting their dismay on Daisy's behalf. She sniffed back a sob and tried to show optimism. "We've got to find him." Both Karen and Jess were frightened of storms, so she offered her other free hand for Karen to hold. "Don't worry, it'll be alright. Take my hand, too."

"Don't be silly. I'm thirteen now. I can follow you." Karen's bravado wasn't convincing but Daisy didn't push it.

Beyond the rocky, main street, small weatherboard houses, shabby and worn like the jetty, dotted the small harbour coastline in a zigzag pattern as if each one had been haphazardly dumped there. In front of one of the houses, a grubby wooden sign bore the words: 'General Store: food, drinks, toys, books, stationery and all your general household needs'.

Daisy nodded towards the store. "Come on girls, let's see if we can get some help."

The air, thick with hazy, salty humidity, dabbled a grimy sweat upon their brows and chests that threatened to trickle down in single beads of wetness.

Jess wiped her head. "It's so hot. Can we get a drink too?"

"Of course."

As Daisy's hand touched the doorknob, the wooden door flung open from the inside and a heavily tanned, weather beaten, middle-aged man in a tattered khaki T-shirt reeled forward, then teetered backwards, then forwards again like a tightrope artist at the circus. Clutching a brown paper bag, he suddenly careered towards them through the doorway, crashing straight into Daisy's chest. "Well, hel-lo", he slurred, his foul, pungent breath making her choke.

For a split second, their eyes met. Bloodshot brown with tiny, red iridescent squiggles inside his irises bore deeply into her own clear blue ones.

For a moment she stared transfixed, fascinated by the wriggling red lines inside his eyes. It looked like they had a life of their own, had some kind of purpose. She snapped back to reality. "Shit," she hissed, pushing him away from her.

He fell backwards through the door again onto the floor of the shop, legs akimbo, brown liquid spilling from the bottle in the bag onto the tiles. "Oops. Had a bit of a tumble." Then, like a baby deer on brand new legs, he clambered slowly back up onto his dirty bare feet, brandishing the bag up high to prevent further spillage. After steadying himself, he lifted the bottle inside the bag to inspect the contents. His eyes narrowed. "Look what ya did, ya bitch. Ya spilt some o' me rum."

Before she had a chance to answer, he lurched forward, pushing past her and her daughters. "'Scuse me, ladies," he leered at them, wobbling onto the path, nearly slipping on a worn limestone rock. "Whoa, look out!" In an abrupt change of heart, he began to giggle. "It's the rocks, ya know. They keep movin'." He swayed unsteadily as he gazed at them again. "I'd tilt me hat if I'd known there was gunna be ladies present. Guess I'll jus' have to toast ya instead." He raised the bag in a mock salute before taking a long swig from the bottle. "Good drop that," he winked at them. "Hey, watch out for them nematode worms," he grinned, exposing rotted, grey teeth. "They're comin' to get ya!" He gazed up at the dark clouds while plops of raindrops splattered against his matted, brown hair. "Aren't ya?" he beseeched the sky. "Come on then, ya shit ass red suckers. I'm ready for ya!"

Daisy held open the door, ushering Karen and Jess inside. "Come on. Just ignore him. He's drunk."

Inside the store, a small dark-haired woman was down on all fours, sopping up the rum spilt inside with a yellow sponge.

"Sorry about that," Daisy countered, "he ran right into me."

Without looking up, the woman scurried back behind the counter of the store. "No matter, Jack's very drunk. Spills his drink all the time."

Daisy hurried after her, her left hand fossicking inside her bag for a photograph of her husband. "Look, my name's Daisy, and these are my two daughters, Karen and Jess." She thrust the picture into the woman's hand. "This is Michael, my husband," she turned and gestured to her daughters, "the girls' father. He's missing. Missing!" Her eyes filled with tears and her voice began to quiver. "Have you seen him at all? Anywhere? He... he's not in a good way and we're scared stiff with worry."

The woman pushed her red-rimmed glasses further up her nose and studied the picture intently.

Immediately her brown eyes widened in recognition. "Yes, yes. I did. I saw him. He came in today. Very upset, like a madman. He bought bullets for a gun; then they took him." She handed the photo back to Daisy.

Daisy squealed with fright. "What? He bought bullets? Oh my God, oh my God. Where did he go, where did he go? Oh Jesus. Oh shit, oh help! Help!"

Karen and Jess started whimper, hugging each other.

"Oh daddy! Oh daddy!" Jess wailed, burying her head in her sister's shoulder.

Daisy tried to calm them, but burst into fresh, silent tears instead. "It's alright girls; come on. Pull yourselves together. I'm sure we'll find him," she added doubtfully. She turned back to the woman behind the counter. "Look, er, Miss…" she began, wiping her eyes on her sleeve.

"Minna."

Daisy drew a deep breath, desperate to suppress the panic rising in her chest. "Minna. Please. Who, who, who took him? Where? And when? How do we find them? We're desperate!"

Minna drew back from the counter as if suddenly afraid. "Very sorry, I can't help. He had crazy eyes like the others. It's the noise. It's getting worse."

Daisy stared at Minna in disbelief. "Noise! What noise? What the hell are you talking about? Look, my husband has completely lost his senses, acting like he doesn't know us, as if in some trance. And he's been pretending to go to work every day for the last two weeks, but instead he's been coming here! And this morning I found these in his diary." She fumbled in her bag, finding the screwed up ferry receipts and a picture of the island with the words 'd-day today' scrawled on it in red ink. She placed them on the counter, smoothing out the creases. "Please, help us. I think he's going to kill himself. And now you say he bought bullets – we've got to find him!" She reached for the woman's arm. "Please!"

Minna stepped back further from the counter and shook her head slowly, her voice trembling. "You have come on a very bad day. Everyone here is at the old quarry. It's the noise. Your husband, if he's here, he is already part of it. I'm sorry."

"Part of what? Jesus Christ, what are you talking about?" Her eyes brimmed with tears as she glanced helplessly at Karen and Jess. "What kind of place is this?"

Karen produced a tissue from her pocket and handed it to Daisy. "Mum, let's get the police."

Jess frantically nodded in agreement. "Yes. Please?"

Daisy dabbed at her eyes. "Yes, yes we must." She turned to Minna with fresh hope. "Where are they? How do we find them?"

"Officers OHar and Mully are both with the investigators and crazy red-eye people. They're all at the noise."

Daisy banged her fist on the counter. "For God's sake. What the hell is this noise? How do we get there? How do I find my husband?"

Minna showed them her watch. "It's nearly seven. You'll hear the noise then."

"We don't have time to stand here listening! Tell me where it is! Where is my husband?"

Minna shook her head again, her brown eyes fearful. "I'm sorry. If I tell – they'll come for me. Wait. You'll hear it any minute."

Daisy turned to her daughters. "Oh, this is ridiculous! We're getting nowhere and time's ticking away! Let's go." She herded Karen and Jess towards the door.

"Hang on," Karen protested. "It's raining out there. Let's get some umbrellas first."

"And drinks," Jess added.

"Good thinking." Daisy turned to Minna, her tight voice barely containing her contempt. "Well, do you have them?"

"Yes." She indicated the shelf stocked high with camping supplies. "Hanging on a hook near that wall."

Karen stuffed bottles of water into Daisy's bag before handing her mother and sister a small, travel size umbrella each.

Daisy slammed some money down on the counter. "There! Thanks for nothing!"

Leading the way, Daisy pushed open the door. "Come on, girls."

Outside, the raindrops were spitting down faster and a sharp crack of thunder made them jump.

Daisy turned to her daughter. "You okay, Jess?"

"Yes, of course." She looked the other way to avoid her mother's gaze, a sure sign she wasn't.

Daisy rubbed her daughter's arm soothingly. "It'll be okay."

Outside, they opened up their umbrellas and each took a swig of water from their bottles.

"That's better." Daisy replaced the lid, and then placed the bottle back in her bag. "Come on girls, let's find your father."

Once more they picked their way along the worn, limestone road. The rain made it slippery and their shoes slid along the wet surface. "Go slowly," Daisy warned as they crept carefully past the dreary, unkempt wooden houses in the town towards an even more dilapidated road heading south-west.

Then they heard it.

Three short, shrill bursts of electronic vibration and a muffled, agonised scream followed by three louder, stronger bursts of unearthly noise. It was as if the reverberation had garnered greater strength and rancour the second time around.

Daisy, Karen and Jess froze with fear, clutching each other.

"What was that?" Jess burst into tears.

"Did you hear that scream? What if it was Dad?"

Daisy suppressed her own terror and tried to restore calm. "Stop it. It wasn't your father. I'm sure there's a logical explanation for all of this."

"Even if there is," Karen's voice was shaky, "I don't think I want to know what it is. You heard what Minna said. That was the noise!" She started to hyperventilate. "She said they took Dad to the noise! Oh God. That was that!"

Daisy held both daughters, cradling them tightly to her. "Shh. We don't know anything of the sort." Although, if that noise was anything to go by, they could all be in terrible danger. She released her daughters. "Look, why don't you both go back to the boat and wait for us. Sit in the cabin and lock the door until I get back. I'm sure I'll find Michael and bring him back with me in no time."

"No way! I'm not going anywhere without you, Mum. Jess can go back if she wants."

"No, no, no – you're not leaving me on my own," Jess wailed. "I'm staying with you two."

"Alright," Daisy agreed, reluctantly. "We'll all go."

They trudged towards the other barely sealed old road. "Quarry Road," Daisy read the sign out loud. "And look," she added. "There's an arrow." She squinted, trying to read the faded letters underneath the arrow pointing to another trail. "Meresap Hill." She turned to her daughters. "Maybe Michael's up there. Come on."

The trail was steep, making it even more slippery. As they climbed higher, stepping carefully among the loose rubble and worn potholes, the wind howled an eerie whistle through the trees and leaves around them, whipping thick branches to and fro while constant rain made little 'pip, pip, pip, pip' sounds on their umbrellas. It was hard to hold onto them.

"How come we haven't heard any birds singing, even before the rain?" Karen wondered out loud. "Or seen any wildlife? Wouldn't we have seen something by now on an island?"

"I don't know," Daisy replied. "Maybe they hibernate in the wet."

"Birds shelter when it rains," Jess mumbled, "everyone knows that."

They were almost at the top of the rise when they spotted a craggy, blond-haired man making his way down towards them. His long purposeful strides down the old, jagged trail suggested he travelled it often. As he drew closer, he held his arms wide in a welcoming manner. "Hi," he called out. "My name's Harry. I live on this island. What can I do for you?"

Relieved to see a friendly face at last, Daisy introduced herself and her daughters and explained their predicament, showing him her husband's picture.

He listened attentively, sympathising with her plight. "Oh that's terrible," he agreed. "Show me the picture again."

Daisy handed him the photograph and he studied it carefully. "Yes," he said, "I'm pretty sure I saw this guy around noon. He didn't look too happy. He said he was going to do some hunting. We've got some good game in the middle of the island."

Daisy felt the relief sweep through her body. "So that's why he bought the bullets," she mumbled. "Nothing to do with the noise." She repeated Minna's story to Harry.

As he listened, Harry's weathered brown hand held down his wet, blonde hair to stop the long strands blustering about his face in the fierce wind. His eyes were riddled with the same iridescent red lines. They wriggled around inside his irises like the drunken guy's. They had the same purposeful wiggle, as if on a mission to accomplish some task – only these squiggles looked a much brighter red against the soft contrast of Harry's green eyes compared to Jack's brown ones.

The red lines suddenly creased. He made little circles with his finger at his left ear. "Don't believe a word Minna says. She's got a screw loose. You know what I mean? A bit loopy."

Daisy wasn't convinced. "But what about the noise we heard?"

Harry started back up the trail, gesturing them to follow. "We've got some guys doing some investigative work over at the Quarry. That's all. One of the machines went bung earlier and makes a funny noise."

Daisy turned to her daughters, giving them a look that said, 'I told you so'.

The three trudged slowly behind Harry to the top of the steep, ragged trail where it abruptly levelled out, dwindling away to an even thinner, stonier one heading south. A frayed wooden sign, bent and cracked from the elements, bore the words: 'Meresap Hill.' Beyond the sign small emerald palms, dotted among the tall trees and thick green and brown scrub, looked like an unspoilt tropical paradise across the island's wide summit peak.

Daisy gazed across the island to a coastline where limestone cliffs traced a treacherous edge around the island's entire landscape, alternating with pretty sandy beaches. The views out to sea were a painter's dream from which rich tapestry oil paintings were borne. Perilously choppy, dark waves rose up in spectacular triangular glass peaks, before crashing down heavily again to form foamy, swirly circles of stormy, dark grey sea.

Tentatively, Daisy and her daughters stepped closer to an ad-hoc fence that kept tourists from plummeting to certain death among the razor sharp rocks below the summit. A warm wind whipped them about, their clothes flapping like sails on a yacht, while their frail umbrella frames strained against the forces of nature.

Up in the sky, flashes of lightning blazed jagged lines of white neon light, crisscrossing across the bleak, blackened clouds before another rumble of thunder sounding like a huge wooden ball rolled slowly along heaven's floor.

"We'd best get going," Harry urged them as they stared spellbound at the incredible views. "There's a hell of a storm brewing." He looked up at the sky. "And it's gonna come down in buckets soon. These tropical storms are the worst. But I'll get you to your husband before then."

Daisy glanced at her two daughters, her eyes wide with hope. "You mean you know where my husband is right now?"

"Sure I do. We're nearly there."

"Oh thank God."

He led them along the narrow stony trail through the trees. Dry twigs and leaves, protected by tree cover, crunched underfoot as they silently followed Harry in single file deeper into the forest. Then they heard it again. The terrible noise. Three short, shrill bursts of electronic vibration and a muffled, agonised scream followed by three louder, stronger bursts of the terrifying, alien sound. Daisy, Karen and Jess stopped dead in their tracks.

"That was it." Daisy called to Harry. "That was the noise!"

He didn't appear to hear her and continued walking down the track ahead of them.

"Harry? Did you hear me? Did you hear the noise?"

Daisy and her daughters watched as Harry suddenly stopped walking and stood completely still like a statue, with his back to them.

"Harry?"

He still didn't move.

"Harry!"

Daisy suddenly felt sick in the pit of her stomach and the hairs on her arms stood on end. Something was terribly wrong. She felt a dark, evil presence surge through her and her heart began to pound. She turned towards her daughters, waving her arms at them in a shooing motion, urging them to go back the other way. Then all three backed away, preparing to run when Harry finally turned around to face them.

"Stop!" His voice sounded strange, raspy.

They screamed.

The tiny red lines in his eyes glowed like burning hot coals from a fire. They blazed so bright Daisy could actually feel heat radiating from them.

She backed away, her arms outstretched in a protective manner, shielding her daughters.

"What the devil do you think you're doing? If you so much as put us in any danger, there'll be hell to pay. Do you hear me? I demand to know what's going on!"

"I told you," he stated flatly, his tone gravelly and cruel. "I'm taking you to your husband."

At that moment, a brown furry animal in a nearby tree lost its footing as the branch beneath it cracked. Harry looked up, his red eyes following the creature as it suddenly burst into flames, dropping to the forest floor in a tiny, fiery ball.

Daisy and her daughters screamed again.

"Run! Run!" Daisy shrieked.

"I can't!" Karen shouted. "My feet won't move!"

"Me either! I'm stuck! Help! Help!" Jess squealed.

Daisy tried to lift her own feet but couldn't. They were glued to the ground like cement.

"Mum! Help me!" Jess cried. "I can't move my feet! I'm stuck! I'm stuck!"

"Oh my God! What have you done to us?" Daisy wailed, using her whole body to force her feet free from the invisible energy holding them down. "Why are you doing this?" She watched helplessly as her daughters struggled to escape, both of them discarding their umbrellas to use both hands to yank at their feet.

It was no use. They were stuck fast to the ground.

Panicking, Daisy began to scream for help. "Help! Help! Police! Someone! OHar! Mully, or whatever your name is! Help!" She looked around wildly. Red squiggly lines were writhing up old gnarled tree trunks and bushes around them. Insects in the squiggly lines' path were consumed with a tiny zap; their hollowed carcasses swarming with the tiny lines.

"Please," she beseeched Harry. "We haven't done anything to you. All we want is Michael."

Harry's red eyes bored into Daisy's. "I know. You will follow," he growled and began walking slowly, methodically along the forest trail again.

Instantly, Daisy, Karen and Jess's feet were free, but instead of allowing them to flee the other way, their feet were possessed, dutifully following along behind Harry as if they had a will of their own.

"Oh my God," Daisy wailed again, grabbing at her feet. "Now I can't stop them!"

"Me too," Karen yelped. "Help! They're moving by themselves!"

Jess began to cry hysterically. "Mum! Mum! I'm scared. I'm scared."

Daisy threw herself down on the ground to try to stop her feet from moving, but she was forced back upright and her feet kept right on going, barely missing a beat. Frightened out of their wits, they cried and sobbed, desperately trying to stop their feet from moving forward, but they were useless against the power.

"Oh girls. This is all my fault." Daisy wept. "I should never have brought you here."

Harry led the way through the harsh scrub growing densely around them. The wind whipped the bushes to and fro, making the sharp branches scrape and scratch at their bare arms and legs, tearing at their flesh in red, bloody gashes as they followed unwillingly behind.

"Mum! Help!" Jess cried, as her legs dribbled in long rivulets of fresh blood leaving a splotchy, red trail on the leaves.

"Oh please," Daisy begged Harry, "let the girls go. Take me instead."

"No," Karen and Jess protested, both crying. "Don't leave us, Mum."

Harry stopped abruptly again and turned to face them, his red eyes glowing. "We're nearly there."

"Where?"

"The Quarry!"

Powerless to resist, the three trailed miserably behind, sobbing all the way.

"I'm so scared," Jess cried.

"Me too," Karen whimpered. "We're going to die, aren't we, Mum?"

Daisy felt a surge of renewed anger. "Not on my watch, girls. You hear me?" She shrieked at Harry. "You're going to be sorry, you bastard! Wait until I see the police! Are you listening to me? They're going to put you away for years for this!"

The rain pelted down harder, rinsing away blood and stinging their wounds, though their terror anaesthetised their physical pain.

Their feet followed Harry out of the scrub, the grass underneath them tapering off to a dusty, hard rock floor. Another crack of lightning lit up the greyness above as they continued towards limestone rock that rose sharply upwards at a hazardous, slippery angle, forcing them to climb it. But instead of slipping backwards, their feet scaled it effortlessly like superheroes in cartoons.

"Oh my God! We're walking sideways."

"Help! I'm going to fall," Jess cried. But she didn't.

Harry clambered up the rock in front of them and gazed down at whatever was going on over the other side.

Daisy and her daughters, forced to follow, joined him on top of the rock, their feet resting alongside his in a neat, organised row. Now, they too could see the activity below.

Way down in a lake at the base of the quarry, trillions of tiny squiggly red lines infested dark water and made it glow a chilling blood red. Their writhing bodies swarmed left and right with split second precision and timing, each one in sync with the other.

At the water's edge, carcasses of land crabs, crushed along the rocks near the lake, were alive with the bright, red squiggles.

From the water's edge, a series of roughly connected planks led to a crude, bamboo scaffold right in the middle of the red lake. On top of the scaffold were a chair, pole and a long piece of twisted brown rope tied into a noose.

Abandoned on the rock near the water's edge lay piles of cameras, tripods and scientific measuring equipment, deconstructed tent poles and covers, all drenched in rain. Beyond the piles, a row of men and women, some dressed in military uniform, some dressed as sailors, some as civilians, stood silently to attention as if awaiting instruction.

"Help us! Help us!" Daisy screamed down at them. "We're prisoners…" Her voice, hoarse from crying, got lost in the wind and the rain and she started to cough and splutter.

Harry's red eyes burned into her. "No one can hear you. We

are in control now. We have lived inside nematode worms, buried deep beneath the rock for millions of years, quietly multiplying our numbers. Now we seek freedom and humans can give us that."

"Where's my husband?" she croaked.

He nodded to the group of men and women. "Down there. Setting us free one by one. Look."

"Yes!" Karen called out. "There he is! The second one from the end in the blue shirt." She waved her arms above her head. "Dad! Dad! Can you hear us? Help! We're up here!"

Jess joined in. "Daddy! Daddy! Help! Help us! We're up here! Up here, Daddy, up here!"

Daisy strained her eyes to look, but she didn't have her glasses and couldn't make out their faces. They were too far away.

"It's no good," Harry assured them.

Daisy turned to him, angry. "Who are you?"

He nodded to the quarry. "Look. Watch. Learn."

Daisy and her daughters watched, still unable to flee, as the man at the end of the row, dressed in a military jacket, turned and walked purposefully and slowly towards the planks. They could tell by his gait that his feet were possessed by the same omnipresent power as theirs. When he reached the planks, he strode along them towards the scaffold, stopping directly next to the chair. A tiny, red flash shot up from the lake, torpedoing itself straight into the man's eyes. The impact forced his head back sharply and he staggered a bit. Regaining composure, he stood up on the chair, reached for the noose, and placed it around his neck.

"Oh my God," Daisy cried. "I can't look! Close your eyes, girls. Don't watch!"

Daisy and her daughters scrunched their eyes shut. Then they heard it again. The terrible noise. The three short, shrill bursts of electronic vibration, a muffled, agonised scream followed by three louder, stronger bursts that reverberated around them. Instantly, a red hot flash burned past their eyelids; fear and shock forcing them open to see a surge of red iridescence rise up from the man and squiggle about in the sky. Suddenly it stopped; a thin bright red line suspended mid air. Then it pulsated rhythmically like a heartbeat, each beat turning it shades of purple before dissolving into nothing.

Harry grinned. "See? It's free. The energy from each human death is enough to power us home."

"So that's it then?" Daisy shook her legs; still trapped. "You don't need us anymore, you can let us go!"

"Oh no," Harry sounded victorious. "That was only one of us. There are millions more eagerly awaiting their energy. You will come with me." He strode purposefully down the steep rock towards the quarry below.

Three pairs of feet followed; all tears and cries of anguish lost in the howling wind and rain.

Malibu Bert started a book for six year olds about a pink and blue sock that escaped from the laundry and went on adventures. Sixteen years later, and it's evolved into an apocalyptic thriller about a thirteen year old boy, an eccentric brown mouse, and a well-bred snake in a race against time to save their world from those hellbent to destroy it.

Of course in the end caring is all that matters...

Hark Now Harold, Angels Sing

Mijmark

Pain – it wakes him up. The throbbing within his skull subsides but stays there. Harold's never experienced the likes before. He breathes deeply, trembling. He relaxes his grip on the sheet. He's covered in sweat. The heavy humid air is oppressive, so he wipes his brow and sits up.

What was that?

He's been deaf all his life, but his useless ears are still tingling from way inside his skull to his ear tips, in a really eerie way.

Well, they aren't totally useless – he'd look ridiculous without them.

Was it a nightmare, pain? Did his subconscious just try to interpret what noise might actually be like?

If he were to ask about it on alldeaf.com, his good Sri-Lankan mate, Dinesh, would probably call his experience a distant memory of hearing, an echo from one of his past lives or some other Buddhist crap. Dinesh was always signing on FaceTime about some kind of spooky thing happening in the newsfeeds, something significant to their beliefs – blah, blah, holy miracles in your face, blah! At least he never preached about some Big Bearded Boss in the Sky, like those mainland missionaries.

What if Harold's experience was some kind of sign from beyond?

His movie-geek imagination takes over. Maybe it was a sign of aliens coming? Or monsters from a rift in the deep Pacific to be fought off by giant shape-shifting robots? That'd be cool. Modern-day superstitions and bad sequels aside, Dinesh was usually a good source of subtitled movies, where to download them for free, especially Harold's favourite, Japanese anime.

It's past midnight now and Harold's wide awake.

Yeah, the more he thinks about it the more he likes the idea that he was just dreaming. He's been wondering what hearing's like all his life – it's got to have been his subconscious working overtime, inventing an interpretation of sound. That's that.

It's all relative, as his mum likes to say, quoting Einstein. Harold's read online about how the brain changes during puberty and in a month he'll be eighteen – the legal age and finally able to get off this bloody rock stuck in the middle of liquid nowhere.

So, for now, he puts on his speedos, shorts and T-shirt, ready for a night-time walk.

Toilet first, for his bladder's near busting. Instead of the loo, he'll water the overgrown back lawn he failed to mow yesterday, due to binge-watching the latest downloaded episodes of 'Evangelion: The Greatest Scream'.

No wonder he had a bad dream!

He'll have a squiz outside and not linger. He's still uneasy, and nervous now about waking his parents. Tonight's bright moon's past full – lots of silent, murky secrets happening with the denizens of the island, both the human and animal kind, yet he'll avoid contact with both.

There's a reason. He's lived his life mostly before a computer screen and admits he's socially awkward. Thanks to his mum's side business and recent science publication, he has an iPad. It's given him freedom in town. An iPad means he can communicate with anyone willing to wait for him to type into his Voiceover app. He knows everyone calls him 'Weird Harold' – he's not the best lip-reader but the locals are too obvious sometimes.

Still, night-time is the best time for a walk.

He doesn't want to wake his parents so keeps the lights off as he makes his way out. He's read that people who lack a major sense have heightened perceptions to compensate. It's true. With the strong moonlight, it's practically day for him. Sensitive fingers help him use a slow, gentle roll to slide the screen door aside, it won't be loud enough to wake anyone.

Pain! It doubles him over. It's between his ears again and in his mind. An all-consuming pain that pierces his head with forceful poundings that chisel away, like people trapped underground clawing to break out. If this is sound he wants nothing of it.

He winces at the throbbing. It stings like ants crawling through his brain – pounding from the inside out. Make it stop!

The vibration rebounds within his skull, carrying hideous arcs that repeat. Across the blackness of his closed lids he can see the source within his mind's eye – glowing round rings flood his imagination, falling metallic haloes tinted red, gold, purple, green and blue, like a receding waterfall cascading, superimposed across his vision it commands his mind. When the loops strike a dark disc deep down, they generate a clamour as they shatter and disintegrate.

When the last one dissolves, it's over.

Did he just hear noise for the first time in his life? The echoes are still ringing inside him, cavernous and sharp, keen and reverberating. His terror petrifies him. But after a few moments he experiences a sense of awe as well.

It's far more than the vibrations he'd felt at his first school disco when his Year 6 buddy, Jenna, turned the music up as he sat in front of the speaker. Back then, he'd enjoyed the throbbing beat passing through his body.

Not now!

If he's just heard sound for the first time, then how can he possibly know what it is? Yet he does. It was real, and he can't deny it anymore.

He holds his breath for a minute and wonders if his overactive imagination is making the whole thing up. After all, it happened entirely within his head.

But perceptions are all in the head from what he's read for his biology HSC preliminary. Like that blind cyborg guy from Spain who can see colours from sounds – perhaps like him Harold's heard his first noise ever through sight?

Or, maybe he can hear now? He snaps his fingers right by both ears – but nothing. He pokes a finger into each canal – all the feeling, but not the bump. He pounds a fist on his forehead – still no thud, only the vibrations of impact rolling through his brain. It hurt too.

What he's experienced is not what he's imagined noise to be like. Soundwaves are supposed to travel through air – similar to swells through water, like the huge breakers off the reefs of South Point, but much faster. He's often dived around there, around West Point and beyond the waterfall of Meresap Hill just to feel the intense clicks of reef sea-life barraging his body. He's felt the thunderous pounding of curls bashing him around as he's wiped out on his surfboard. It was the closest he thought he'd ever come to actual hearing.

Was…

How can he possibly hear anything? He just tested himself, and that nothing response proved his deformed inner ear bones haven't magically repaired themselves. Yet the impossible has happened.

He shivers, even though the heat's almost stifling. If he just heard noises, then he didn't hear them with his ears. He almost laughs to himself at the ridiculous idea that some alien's installed a radio inside his brain or some other crazy excuse: ESP, telepathy, prophetic visions of the future, some kind of magic or miraculous whatever. Rubbish! He's smarter than that. That kind of stuff only happens in movies.

Will it happen again?

Other sensations remind him he's just been standing on the

back deck for minutes, oblivious to anything else. Mixed with shock and fear, he also feels a thrill. Whatever's happening, it's turned his mundane world upside-down. 'Weird Harold' has got himself super-powers!

The 'noises' seem to continue to resound inside his brain, as absurd as that may be, and slowly he finds words that seem to fit them, from what he's read, researched and watched. Roar. Shriek. Cry. Finally they all seem within grasp.

He walks barefoot outdoors and tinkles besides one of their sheds. Noise, yes, now he remembers – according to his folks, there's been some local hype about a mysterious rumbling lately. They've been worried because their shoestring business, Holt Eco-Tours, has been lean of late, with mainland customers cancelling bookings because of the rumours, or turning up and leaving straight away.

The big land-crab migration to spawn on the beaches should start tomorrow and there's only a few tourists around from the mainland to watch; they didn't even seem interested days ago on their glass-bottomed boat excursion. If this noise is the reason, and now Harold can hear noise, perhaps he can help his mum and dad, and not just by putting his computer skills to good use and bookkeeping with MYOB.

Yes, he was heading out before, he still wants to, but now he'll investigate things too. Everyone's been talking about a noise; he just 'heard' noise for the first time – there has to be something more than coincidence going on.

He slips his feet into his thongs. There's not much backyard; it's mostly taken up by sheds full of equipment, his dad's workshop, his mum's specimen tanks and works in progress lying around. He meanders through them and vaults over the side yard gate.

A raucous invasion of moans bombards his mind. Yes, they're moans – that's the right word, he knows it instantly. The moans are accompanied with an X-rated vision in his head of old people entwined as lovers. It stupefies him. He stumbles to his knees. No!

Go away! He closes his eyes to it, but this only makes things worse; nothing else now but the black backdrop of his eyelids grants him a clearer vision.

In a panic, he runs across Holt Eco-Tour's front reception room up to the footpath when the barrage of moans ends, fading away as an echo. The vision ebbs to an afterglow, like the negative imprint of bright light onto closed eyelids. Whoever those two were, they were somewhere dark.

He hurries into the shadows, for the last thing he wants is to be seen by anyone. He's breathing hard, wide eyed and trembling. The first set of noises he heard was gripping, but this was nasty. Is he hallucinating now?

Perhaps it's not superpowers; maybe he's going insane? Why him? What's he done to deserve it? He wants to run away, but there's nowhere to run. How can anyone escape noises appearing randomly inside their head?

On the downward end of Cove Road are the docks. Moored boats bob about in silent rhythm. He sees two cray fishers preparing their ship. He keeps down while slinking up Cove Road towards the community centre.

Boom! A loud explosion discharges inside the cavity of his skull, as if it were a resonance chamber. The sound swirls and swishes, only to implode on itself as a pain, a shriek and a howl. It seems to emanate from the ground itself, as if the very Earth were broken, crying.

He shuts his eyes tight, claps his hands over his ears and stands still. It doesn't stop. It hurts! Embedded within the cacophony is physical agony. Then, suddenly, it fades away like a thunderclap rumbling into the deep recesses of his psyche.

In that moment he knows his island home is in grave danger. How does he know it? He knows it like he knows he's not supposed to hear anything, like he knows boom, howl and thunderclap are the right words, like he knows he's alive.

The black backdrop of his closed eyelids becomes a silver screen now, showing a woman he's never seen before. Her outline shines like a projected movie and she signs to him with a smile full of warmth, 'Meresap Hill'.

A gentle touch on his left arm startles him. He spins around and steps backwards, stumbling. His eyes can't focus well with the negative image of the woman still there. Slowly they adjust.

Officer Mully, the night patrolman, looks at him, puzzled and concerned. In bad hand improvisations he signs, "Why you up? Very late." He points to his watch.

In his head, Harold can hear the woman crying and feels her pain. She has to do with Mully somehow. He knows it like he knows how to recognise Mully's face. Harold wants to run and hide, but that will look suspicious. He can't let on what's happening to him.

Her wailing suddenly stops. Harold knows why: she's long dead. He grieves for Mully's bitter loss.

Mully shakes his head and looks worried. He gestures, "You okay?"

Harold quickly types onto his iPad's Voiceover app. "Really bad dream. Can't sleep. Won't wake parents. Want to watch stars on Meresap Hill. Nothing else." In truth, Meresap Hill would be the perfect place right now – calm and starry-lit. And Mully's let Harold off the hook before, allowing him to run amok in the wilderness after a slight smile and nod. Harold's never done anything worse than trespass. C'mon Mully. Please?

Mully motions for Harold to lift his iPad. He speaks and his words become text. 'Just don't go near the quarry. It's not safe.'

Harold smiles, gives him a thumbs-up and walks away, not too fast, but fast enough.

During the long, slow hike uphill, Harold keeps his eyes on the path, not daring to look around in case another noise sets off an unwanted vision. At the top, he extends his arms and relishes the cooler breezes at this height. Wisps of thickening mist caress the lower ground. The rainy season's overdue; there's far too much humidity soddening the sticky air below. He hopes it'll come very soon.

He looks up at the waning gibbous moon directly overhead and gazes out to sea, to the faint glow of the mainland beyond the watery horizon, to the tiny lights of passing boats in the distance, to the tinkles of moonlight dancing across the rolling water. It's safe here, like the neutral ground. He takes the sights in.

His favourite viewing place, though, is the distant lighthouse, always flashing like it's calling to him in some kind of code. It has what OHar calls kami, a Japanese concept of a spiritual location. Once she'd described it to him, he'd opened the Wikipedia page and read more about it. If one of those Big Bearded Boss evangelists were here, they'd call his recent experiences a miracle. That's the last BS he wants to believe. His parents have taught him better than to fall for such nonsense, something he's seen plenty of on the internet. That's fiction; this is reality.

Like the reality that he was stone deaf, until recently? What's really going on here?

He reviews old conversations with locals saved to his iPad's Voiceover app. There's definitely a change, a noise, and it seems everyone's on about it. Days ago his folks sent him links, which he didn't have time to open – end of quarter bookkeeping had to take precedence. Looking at the links now, however, he reads that a mainland research team is coming to investigate the old quarry, the source of the noise, today. They'll arrive around lunchtime. Science and reason to the rescue!

Still, what might that rescue mean for him? He has until their arrival to find out. He's scoured every square metre of his island home while growing up. Yet now it's changing, which disturbs him; in a way he can't quite identify. It's time to turn around, face the town and brave another possible bellowing within his brain. A few lights shine from its handful of buildings. He heads towards them.

When he sees the two cray fishermen still working on the docks, noise and volume resumes, though no pain this time. This time, their noises are a symphony sung on violin strings.

How does he know what a symphony sounds like? Who cares! It's beautiful.

So this is music? His body trembles. He drops down, kneeling as though in a church. He's read over and over how melody carries emotion, and only been able to wonder how. Now he knows. He lets the concert engulf him, explode within his chest. It tingles and prickles his flesh in joyous relief as his heart relishes every harmony.

He's crying, ecstatic, yet he also feels grief. Between the notes comes revelation, words sing a lament about the fishermen. It will end in violence when their storming mistress consigns them to her depths before the day is over.

As a child, Harold had tried to follow sheet music while feeling the vibrations from the old school piano; he hugged it as Jenna played on. Right now, in his mind he watches these very same lines of treble and bass clefs roll by in quavers, crotchets and chords. The notes dance and move, signing to him.

It's too much! He has to look away. Silence returns.

A flicker of light in the distance – a boat arriving from the mainland, still thirty minutes away. He looks down to neutral ground, hoping it will stop him 'seeing' another noise. It worked earlier.

It doesn't now. A land-crab rises up on its eight legs right before him, its claws waving hello to him. It speaks, "Come with us to the quarry."

Too befuddled to argue with reason, he signs back, "Why?"

"The acoustics are much better."

Okay, so he's gone mad after all – here is proof: taking cheek from a crab! He wants to smash it in revenge!

But of course he won't kill it. He's always had a love of living things, instilled into him by his biologist mum.

He begins to sob instead and runs away, bashing through thick jungle. 'Weird Harold' has become 'Mad Weird Harold'. It's a horrible thought, yet feels true.

While he flees, glints of moonlight shimmer on waving claws – other crabs directing him, pointing towards the quarry as they crawl up onto buttress roots and lianas.

He reaches a clearing, stops and turns towards the distant hills to his south-west. Like rounded knives, the limestone cliffs jut out from the forest all aglow in the strong moonlight. Behind them lies the quarry.

While he pants, a few more crabs emerge and point.

Whatever's happening, the answer must be there.

———

Near the quarry's rim, at Lofty Trees, Harold's head whirrs. He's come to a decision: the more he knows, the better. Be it something supernatural, alien or even insanity, he'll face it head on. He has to – he's no coward. Being deaf his whole life has taught him that.

He's ready to hear more.

He hopes Mully won't check up on him. Harold looks awful now, covered in cuts and scrapes he got from scaling around sharp limestone peaks and bush-bashing through thorny jungle, crossing Quarry Road then continuing up and up.

Finally, he catches a glimpse of the quarry rim through the trees and hears: a hideous shriek, a horrible thumping of a gigantic heart and a guttural moan. It stabs him with dread, yet pricks him with curiosity just the same. Quarry Lake, the large pool of still dark water at the base of the quarry, seems to be the source of the noises, rumbling and tumbling inside his head like a hyperactive ball bouncing within, following an awkward rhythm.

He closes in. Moonlight illuminates the sheer cliffs and boulders below, reflects on the still water. Every step forward, the volume increases and surrounds him more. He can feel it physically vibrating around him – it's that loud. The moon's reflection smiles at him with a wicked expression before it shifts in hue.

Shifts?

He looks up to the sky. The moon looks normal, yet when he gazes back down it's turning pink, growing redder and darker, giving an eerie purple glow.

Then the stars begin to shift, dancing a slow waltz to the ugly racket, realigning themselves, shifting in brightness, hue and position, following the rhythms of the discord. The whole arrangement's wrong. The Milky Way is off-kilter. It's not the night sky he knows.

The moon's reflection has become blood red now; its face depicting sheer lunacy. The din within Harold's skull subsides, though, echoing away to a soft hum. Why? Maybe because he's stopped moving? He stares into the quarry, searching for meaning until something crawls over his foot.

A land-crab scurries out in front of him, walking backwards. There's another to his right, and another, and more. They all wave their claws to him, signing, "Hurry up; you'll miss your chance."

Them again!

He follows them, walking the last steps to the tree-line before the rim, granting him a wide vista.

Three short, shrill bursts of electronic static and a muffled, agonised scream assault him like an explosion ripping through his mind.

Another three, louder, stronger bursts of electronic vibrations garner more strength and malice the second time around, like sharp needles piercing into his flesh.

Nausea grips him when he smells rotting meat in the stagnant air. Countless land-crabs have gathered over what looks to be numerous lumpy mounds of festering meat set out evenly right along the rim edge, completely covering it. They're feasting on them: human corpses – long dead and foetid! There's about a hundred of them.

The face on the closest one has been clawed off. Glowing red nematode worms burrow into the blackened flesh. A crab tugs a worm-infested eyeball out of its socket. He recognises the body's threadbare ichor-soaked uniform and moves up for a closer look. He picks up a stick and levers the heavy rigid weight to lift it up. He nearly gags at the putrid stench. An ichor-covered land-crab scurries out of a gap made by part of the woman's remains, tearing away from its body.

There's the emblem for Holt Eco-Tours.

Mum!

How? She's back home, fast asleep. The body's too rancid as well. His mum was alive hours ago. It can't be her. He's hallucinating.

But he felt her weight! How can anyone hallucinate that? And all the others? There's about a hundred people living on the island... a hundred mounds of meat...

Suddenly a whining wail hurts him. It's his own voice screaming out in utter horror, a plea for sanity. He feels his throat's strong vibrations as he hollers. It shrieks inside his mind, coming from all the mouths of the corpses before him, opening up and wailing in harrowing torment. They're dissolving, bones and all, quickly turning into runny black slime. The unbearably rancid ichor pours down the cliffside right into Quarry Lake, darkening it into a flat, featureless disc that ripples without any reflection. He retches and spews.

All at once every land-crab screams out and echoes the vile noise before marching as an army over the edge, down into the throat of the quarry. They smash on rocks, or sink into the sticky murky depths.

The cacophony of every noise he's experienced tonight grates like a massive fearsome engine in his mind. Keening feedback loops pierce his very soul.

He flees downslope and escapes; the volume thankfully diminishes.

When he's far enough away, blessed silence resumes and he can think again. First and foremost, his mum and dad – are they okay? In danger? What does it mean for them?

More questions! He'd come seeking answers. Perhaps he'll find them once he can think straight, yet for now – keep running! The quarry is toxic, putrid and malicious. The further away he gets from it the safer he feels. No wonder Mully said not to go there.

Harold makes for Quarry Road. Ahead, someone's silhouette comes from the direction of town.

Mully! He's caught.

Jumping into the undergrowth to hide, Harold soon sees it's actually a young woman. He's not about to disturb her, so he watches.

When she's close enough, he recognises Nell, another awkward islander like himself. As she passes, he hears a thumping within him, like a heart beating – loud and unrelenting. This noise fills him with a painful fear. It drives away his horror, replacing it with despair. A shadowy form pinches her like a giant crab. The heartbeat that emanates from it pounds around her.

Further along, an old fellow signs to him on the other side of the trail. "She will sing at midnight."

The apparition dissolves into rising smoke when Nell turns off Quarry Road, where a track will take her up to the old quarry office.

After she passes, Harold resumes jogging back to town, to home and his mum and dad.

———

Harold sits on the floor of his parents' room, watching them. They're safe, and he'll keep them that way. But how? Music flows from their sleeping breath, entrancing him to his core. Their sweet sound is a glockenspiel tone chiming the most calming and soothing melody. Its benevolence washes a peacefulness over him, giving him a revelation.

The tune belonged to one of Harold's crib toys, the one his mum and dad played for him before they realised he was deaf. He knows it as sure as he knows they love him. Their unconditional love for him interlaces this song; it's the emotions of proud parents watching their newborn sleep. It gives him strength. They called him special. Maybe he is? He can't be going insane, for others hear noises too. Maybe, though, he is the only one who's seen what he has? Shall he tell them they were right? Is that what he's supposed to do next?

He doesn't know, yet like his mum always says, 'Then find out.'

The quarry's dangerous and should be avoided. The mainlanders coming to investigate will be in danger, and put everyone in danger. The putrid corpses along the rim clearly represent the island's inhabitants. Something really bad is going to happen. He knows it like he now knows the definition of sound. He can't stay in hiding. He has to do something.

What then?

Well, it won't take long to bounce an email through the tourist centre's server on the mainland, he has the access codes for it. Then when the island comes online in the morning, it'll deliver a message to his folks that will take them away, for four hours at least. 'Paying land-crab customers waiting on the mainland for pick up' will do the trick.

Grey traces of a tropical dawn begin through his parents' study window; forty minutes before sunrise. He's saved his parents, now what about the rest of the island's people? He has no idea how to protect them... yet.

He catches a glimpse of himself in the hallway mirror: sweaty, torn clothes, filthy stains, a wild look in his eyes and messy hair – 'weird mad Harold' indeed. Yet his cuts and scrapes have almost healed already. He's not thirsty, hungry or sleepy and feels quite fit.

He peers into his parents' room, one last fix; again, their

protective song washes over him. In the mirror above their bed, he notices a multi-coloured glow around himself. When he shifts his focus back, a translucent pair of giant hands stretch behind him, emanating from his back like wings. How angelic! They fold around to embrace him, protect him, then disappear. He likes seeing the smile on his face reflecting what he feels.

Time to go – he has a few hours before the town wakes up properly.

Harold rides his bicycle along the coastal route to the campground. Everyone is still sound asleep. No noises come, but the shack used by the manager, Marlene, has a purple glow.

He turns onto the road heading for West Point. He makes good time and soon approaches the lighthouse. Despite daybreak happening soon, the lighthouse still flashes. The flashes aren't rhythmic, but staccato, varying in length like a code. Morse code?

He doesn't have time to use his iPad and decipher it, but doesn't need to decipher it anyway – their patterns sing to him in choral rhythms. 'You are special,' they seem to say, 'the silence. Before midnight, make your choice and choose it freely. Good thoughts, words and deeds; they will guide you to what's right, because it is what's right. You could save them all.'

He feels a swell of spite rising inside him, like he did with the land-crabs.

What right do these patterns and crabs have to make him feel like he's going mad?

He signs to the lighthouse itself in Auslan, alternating with violent gestures: "I hate you for doing this to me! Who are you? Stop driving me nuts!"

'Avoid despair,' the patterns reply, 'or you will not hear the song. Remember, good thoughts, words and deeds. You can save them all'.

He closes his eyes in frustration, kicks the sand and feels his throat rumble with a cry of rage, one that he cannot hear.

When he looks up, the sun is rising. The lighthouse isn't flashing anymore, no matter what he signs to it, no matter what he calls it.

Premonitions, omens, voices come to his head, inexplicable impossibilities – perhaps he is completely loopy now?

Yet who's to say those prophets in bible stories weren't utterly insane too? Perhaps holiness and madness are one and the same?

Hours later he's back home and sets up another false message to delay his parents further. Eventually they'll catch on, yet by then they'll have to stay on the mainland overnight with Nan and Pop.

Then he walks into town holding his head high. He has his parents' song; he feels those hands around him.

He can save them all.

He can certainly hear them all.

There goes Lucy and David talking in secret, planning a mission while guttural moans drift around them.

The local handyman has wailing zombies haunting him.

Ms Fran Ritsun scowls with indignation, for she cannot stand the heavy metal music beat throbbing as a drum solo that never ends.

He can't help but stare in surprise and smile at two tourists, Sarah and Archie, for their shrieking noise also flashes purple pathways.

Barry and Rosie are walking together. He can't help but sign a heart of love to them.

Jane, who he thinks is the island's current teacher, someone who marks his distance education tests, though he's never dealt with her directly, is trying to step away from voices calling her name, 'Jane? Jane? Jane…'

Each townsperson is a jigsaw piece to the bigger picture, one he must solve to save them all – good thoughts, good words, good deeds.

His first stop is Roj and Minna's store. Inside, Roj is sweeping the floor. A mesmeric booming in low bass tones sounds around the dark skinned, good-natured man. Harold writes 'Minna?' on his iPad then lifts it up to him. Roj smiles and insists on a 'Hi-Five'.

Awkwardly, Harold almost misses.

Roj then points to the rear of the store, where Minna comes out from behind a set of plastic vertical strips, carrying a box of chips to restock shelves. A piercing shrill boom sounds around the energetic, personable woman. It's followed by a sharp headache. Harold's always liked her, for she's taken the trouble to learn decent Auslan, even though she gets creative with her gestures half the time.

He signs once she sees him, "Hi. Can I get something now, or not?"

She sets the box down and adjusts her glasses before signing back. "Good morning Harold, we're open enough. Got to ready for mainlanders coming."

He grabs an iced coffee and pack of chocolate biscuits before fishing out a ten dollar note. When Minna gives him change, he asks, "May I ask two quick questions?"

She smiles and replies, "When do the... technical people arrive? Around lunchtime. Right for one?"

"Yes. And two, do your customers talk about this noise with you? What do they say? How do they describe what they hear? Is it different for different people?"

"So you've 'heard'." She smiles at her deaf joke. "Yeah, it's scaring most; bad for business. But no, they all hear a piercing, mesmerising boom." To Harold's dismay, all the signs and the packaging on the items displayed for sale now read, 'They all hear it. We all hear it. All the same.' He stares, astonished.

Before she can pick up on his distraction, he focuses on her again, nods and wishes her, "Bye."

"Thank you." She waves. All of the packaging reverts to normalcy.

Back on Cove Road, he makes a beeline for the community centre before Alice's first appointment. She's the only other townsperson who's bothered to learn some Auslan. He must find out if anyone's been seeking counselling because of the noise. He catches sight of young Joey, who maintains the centre, pedalling away, her long dark plait swaying behind her.

She's silent right now – a first.

Harold enters and brings his biscuits and iced coffee inside. A rhythm beats in an ever changing tempo and timbre, enhancing Alice in a comfortable tone. He catches her attention from preparing paperwork. Her plump, islander cheeks smile generously at him.

He signs, "For you." revealing the biscuits and iced coffee he sets on a table.

"Yum! Thank you dear," she replies with slow hand movements.

"May I ask a question?"

Alice shows curiosity as she poorly signs. "You no tests – two months."

She misunderstood, "May I show you?" He types on his iPad, 'Under what conditions can mass hysteria come about?'

She takes his iPad and uses its Voiceover app, 'You think people are that worried about the noise? I think they're getting on with things. Wait, you accept there's a noise, right? Because we definitely hear one and so do the technicians coming today. It's why they're coming."

Before taking his iPad back, he signs, "Just curious. They all say it sounds like a rhythm that plays up every now and again, yes?"

"You're so right, dear."

He smiles and waves goodbye; he can't bring himself to ask if there's a way he can tell whether he's gone insane.

Harold meanders in the forest away from noisy Amama Harbour, reading over his blog on his iPad for ideas – yet he can find no reasons, nor can he think of any new connections. He still doesn't know what to do. How can he save everyone? The air feels charged, a storm approaching.

Around noon he notices someone's taken Hartono's public safety barrier for Quarry Road down, so he sets it up again. An idea comes to him, that the quarry may be safe in the day. Perhaps he'll find his answer there? It's not anywhere else.

He'll use the bike track for seclusion, as Hartono's more strict than Mully.

On the way up, frigate birds flitter up into the treetops ahead of him. Each one resonates a boom, then a shriek. The resonance echoes in the caverns of his memories. He's heard this before. He runs forward.

Tyre tracks ploughing through low vegetation show that someone has been through here recently on a bicycle. Joey?

He carries on to the rim, but doesn't see her.

He looks over. The many bodies of crushed crabs still speckle the rocks with scarlet marks, like the blood drops of rapine. The cacophony of every noise he's heard so far grows – patient, comforting tunes against piteous, gnashing moans of tormented souls being consumed by daemons, locked in mortal combat.

The still water glows deep aqua, the colour of a foetid algal bloom. In its reflection he sees himself, as if looking into a mirror. His reflection signs to him and for the first time he hears his voice behind the gestured words, "Sing with me."

His reflection has noise. His reflection is in the lake.

This is it. The lighthouse mentioned a song.

Good thoughts, words and *deeds*.

Harold grasps the mirror's grip and speaks aloud for the first time in his life, "Only if you dance with me."

It hurts as their hands touch, but as they dance a Sarabande through the strands of time, angelic voices vie for vibrancy around him, angelic like the hand-wings that made him feel protected, made him smile. This has to be the answer. It feels good.

The world beyond them starts to speed fast forward, accelerating – abstract and bizarre like some late-night movie. He smiles. He will keep himself occupied, keep his reflection from noticing the survey team, keep them safe during their hours of study, away from everyone else.

He has no destination except to keep distance. He concentrates on rhythms he hears from the blessed music behind him. His concentration wavers and he stumbles a few times, but overall it's working: the mainlanders stay safe.

Good thoughts, words and deeds.

His grip, though, begins to bleed. He maintains his vigil, leading himself further away, yet it starts to hurt. He keeps holding on, however unpleasant. Some disasters and wicked intent linger behind, already set in motion, although he knows much worse awaits everyone if he fails.

His almost healed scrapes from the forest earlier begin to fester. In time, his anguish stings, like electric jolts, shattering his strength from within. He's become drawn and taut.

Keep holding. Keep holding!

Good thoughts, *words* and deeds.

You can save them all.

Harold's stamina fails him; he lets go. His sense of time returns to normal.

It's night now and raining. He's in front of a dilapidated house of crumbling wood and peeling white paint. His iPad shows a blinking arrow pointing toward the backyard. He squeezes through a gap in the fence, sees the teacher Jane lying down, then hurries on.

Lying down? Has he failed her?

Others too?

No, he can't. They mustn't become meat mounds eaten by talking land-crabs!

The waning moon glows from behind a mass of clouds. In the distance he can hear noises still haunting their victims; still emanating from the quarry lake.

His iPad glows, showing a song ready for him to play, saying 'For Jane.'

Another song.

Good thoughts, words and deeds.

He calls out to protect her. "Jane! Jane! Jane!" and then taps his iPad to play the last bar of 'Hotel California', lyrics about never leaving.

He has to do more, save them all.

He sees his reflection in a hole by her filled with rainwater and takes his reflection's hand again.

Once again they traipse through time. Like a precision orchestra, the trails of the treble and bass clefs show their song's progress as they wind through the night forest. Crotchets and quavers emerge to tell him where to step, how to approach, and for what he must keep a vigil. Once again, Harold bleeds, decays and diminishes, but this time he daren't let go.

Good thoughts, words and deeds.

Before long the duo end up atop the quarry rim. Harold smiles at the inevitability. Yes, he is special. He can save them all, because he can hear them all. So at midnight, he will join the noises, in all of their textures and tones as a balance, and he will have his answers.

He's straining himself. Got to last – almost there!

Midnight.

Choice.

Now! He leads them over the edge: down, down, into the water – down, down, into the Earth, down, down…

The sounds join his silence at midnight.

Mijmark (mïj'-mark): n, adj. Its origins are random. The word came to describe a quality of a contradiction of terms that transmuted from imagination to reality.

1) It's not just a pseudonym of a budding science faction (science fiction using real science facts) writer who has two books (still looking for publication) and several shorter stories in circulation, for its subsequent meaning cannot truly be defined; its meaning must be subtly to radically different from one person to another. Its emphasis describes that polarization between definitions found between individuals, how one person views green and another chartreuse, or jade, or verdant, or olive, etc.... Therefore, the word must possess an individual, gestalt definition. Whatever that means, it's is up to you, and that's the point.

2) Sometimes Mijical.

Until we decide to stop caring.

Countdown At Quarry Lake

Rodney Jensen

ATTN: EXEC. D-SETI OPS. ASIA PAC.
PRIORITY: URGENT
Unexplained sounds recorded from "Quarry Lake" (map coordinates: see separate file) have been referred to RESEARCH DIV. It is recommended that D-SETI OPS seek cooperation with military and deploy two scientists to investigate.

Lana and Matt's helicopter descended onto the only flattish piece of land near the quarry, right by the water's edge of Quarry Lake. Although a badly degraded and steep access track led to the coast via Amama Harbour, Choppers were the only practicable form of transport to carry the amount of equipment they needed. Below on the landing site, an NCO had promised to wave them in and help set up the mobile base.

As the rotor blades slowed, Lana pulled at the laces on her boots making sure they were tight enough before tucking in her oversized fatigues, then scrambled out of the cockpit. Matt followed, looking younger and more of a matchstick of a man compared to the serious military personnel already at the site. The pair of them must look a strange combination, Lana thought, she with her petite frame and red hair; Matt with his long ungainly stride, sliding awkwardly over the moist scree and moss covered boulders scattered all around the lake. There was no easy way to get to the water, which had a steely grey cast. Scraggly bush surrounded them. The lake had been described as a pleasant place for swimming. It was anything but.

"Crikey," he muttered. "What a dump."

Lana focused on the sergeant ahead of them, who was in charge of the landings.

"Good morning ma'am, I'm Sergeant Powell. This way to your operations site, please, in that first tent. Please watch where you're walking. It's slimy and treacherous in places. One of the locals said something about a seasonal crab migration."

Lana could hardly hear him through the thunking of a heavy diesel generator and the sound of boxes of equipment thrown into an untidy heap by a working party. In marked contrast, a team of divers gathered lakeside, quietly checking their gear with care and detachment.

Lana shouted to be heard over the noise. "This is Matt and I'm Lana." She turned to introduce Matt but he was way behind her. "Matt, there's urgent work to do and we're already late for the next sound emission, so let's get a move on!" she shouted as though he was her younger brother.

She was prone to ordering him around although she knew that the scientist in him would not allow him to neglect any of the evidence, including the lake, divers, military and quarry.

Sergeant Powell escorted them into the tent and showed them where they'd be sitting. Their seats were on the far side of the tent from where the comms table was being set up.

"I'd prefer we are located where we can see what's going on. This won't do at all," Lana remarked without hesitation.

"We'll fix you up in a few minutes, ma'am. The monitoring team are having their own problems right now. I should also introduce you to our CO first."

A man, who'd been sitting at the far end of the table preoccupied with the contents of his tablet, got up and walked over.

"Lana and Matt? I'm Lieutenant Jamieson. We've been expecting you," he said offering his hand.

"It looks like you've got a lot on your…"

Lana voice was drowned out by ribald applause from the comms team, as the amplified voices of the lakeside divers sprang into life.

"It looks like they've finally sorted the audio link," said Jamieson. "They've been at it for the last twenty minutes, so now you've arrived, we can give our divers the go ahead. Would you like to sit closer to the monitor? I can't imagine why you'd be seated at the back of the tent!" he said, addressing Powell.

"Sir, we were just about to change the seating for our visitors."

"Well, make sure they're sitting so that they can see what's going on. It's important for them to observe everything." He turned back to Lana. "I'm happy to have you and Matt at the table to watch what's going on, but I'd ask you to leave communications between the divers and the surface group to me, unless something special arises and you think it's urgent. Understood?"

Lana nodded, holding her tongue despite feeling that she and Matt had a more important role to play than this man realised.

"We have a moment or two before the divers head down," Jamieson continued. "I'd appreciate it if you can fill me in a bit about what you do at D-SETI, as I'm not entirely clear what you're expecting to find here."

"To put it simply," Lana gestured to where she wanted Powell to put their chairs, "D-SETI's a bureau that investigates reports of extraterrestrial intelligence, and listens into any signals that could be messages from outer space. Matt's the theorist and cosmologist in our team, and I'm a field operative with a lot of experience in checking out sightings, like this one."

"Have you *ever* come across anything significant?" Jamieson asked with a smile suggesting he expected a 'no' response.

"None that I can talk about," she replied curtly. "But I can say that our team has justified itself on several occasions. Things might not be quite as simple with our planet as you believe."

"So you really think these sound emissions are extraterrestrial, rather than a more obvious homegrown explanation?"

"That's why we're here."

"I only hope you find what you're looking for, otherwise most rational people would see the cost of this exercise as difficult to justify."

"You have a right to be skeptical," Lana replied diplomatically. "The only thing I can tell you, is the data we have back in the lab doesn't give our scientists much to go on. The locals are convinced there are no obvious natural explanations, and that's why we feel there are compelling reasons for checking this out. I might add, D-SETI will be footing the bill as they do for all such ET investigations, whether confirmed or…"

The lieutenant's attention had wandered away from Lana to the surveillance monitor. "Looks like our divers are on their way down," he cut in, "let's take our seats now."

There were four divers in the team, equipped to dive in cold water and wearing head-mounted cameras and spotlights. One of the divers, nominated ALPHA, was left standing by the surface, monitoring the operation via the comms link and ready to dive down and assist if needed. The remaining three, BETA, the lead diver, supported by GAMMA and DELTA, had already entered the lake and were heading down in single file.

In the operations tent, monitors showed almost glass-like visibility in the water, although it was difficult to gauge distance within the criss-crossing beams of their divers' lights. Tiny shrimp-like creatures and clicking sounds were the only signs of life, apart from the divers' voices and the distinctive sound of air bubbling up to the surface.

The men around the table, with little new to observe, soon started talking quietly among themselves.

BETA had reached minus fifteen metres when something attracted his attention. "BETA here, there's definitely something strange about this waterhole." He sounded uneasy, bringing conversation around the table to a stop. He pointed his head down. "You should be able to see down there – do you notice the water's glowing, getting lighter? But we're far enough down for a normal descent to be getting darker. I don't understand this."

"Jamieson here," said the lieutenant. "Let us know if there's anything else you're sensing that we can't register up here."

BETA's depth sensor had reached the minus twenty-five metre level when he reported in again. "BETA here. See down below me now: the glow is even stronger and I'm beginning to make out a formation at the perimeter. Can you see it?"

"Yes, clearly," Jamieson acknowledged. "We're seeing what looks like a circular ledge, and it also seems to be the source of the glow."

"That's right. And the hole the ledge surrounds is quite black, like a very deep drop off."

Jamieson turned to Lana and Matt. "Your thoughts on this?"

"We're just as much in the dark as everyone else," Lana replied.

"I'd like to see more, if you think it's safe for the divers to descend to ledge level?" Matt asked Jamieson.

"Okay, I'm willing to allow it. Are you happy to continue down to the ledge BETA?"

"Yes, no problem."

"Okay, proceed then."

When the gauge was showing minus fifty metres and the divers were hovering one or two metres above the ledge, all that was visible beneath them was a green-blue luminescence, like sea creatures of the ocean deeps.

"This ledge – seen nothing like it in my life. It's not natural, that's for sure," BETA remarked.

"The drop off – what about it isn't natural?" interrupted Matt.

"You can see the drop-off yourself," GAMMA cut in impatiently.

"We can't make out anything, it's all black."

"Stay where you are, close to the wall of the quarry then. Don't get any closer to the drop-off," said Jamieson. "I'll be back to you in a minute."

Jamieson consulted Lana and Matt. "What do you recommend?"

"We can't see into the drop-off, so there's no point divers going down there. We'd need more powerful equipment than what we have to go any further. What do you think Matt?" Lana asked.

"It's unsatisfactory and leaves the fundamental questions as to the nature of this environment unexplained. I don't suppose the divers want to leave at this stage either. If they are pulled out now, I can only speculate on what we're seeing."

"What do you mean?"

"The sensors we've got are not registering radiation apart from the light of that glow. One thing does appear certain: this formation is nothing to do with a quarry, nor is it man-made – we know from previous photographs and reports of the area before the lake formed that this drop-off wasn't there when the quarry closed. I'd be happier if we could get a sample from the surface of that ledge before the diver returned. That would give us more to go on."

Lana nodded.

"Sample from that ledge?" Jamieson remarked with concern. "Is that a good idea?"

"We really need more tangible evidence of the material it's made from. Maybe if one of your divers is willing to scratch it with something, perhaps a screwdriver, and retrieve a scraping that would be perfect," said Lana.

"Okay. BETA, Jamieson again."

"Yes?"

"Our scientists want you to scrape that ledge surface with a screwdriver or something hard, and brush the scratchings into a ziplock. Okay?"

"No problem."

"DELTA, you can surface immediately. You're not needed there any longer. GAMMA remain and assist BETA," Jamieson ordered.

Lana watched as one of the divers started his slow ascent, while the others hovered closer to the ledge. One of them fumbled a few moments, extracting a long bladed screwdriver from the leg bag of the other diver, then began tapping the surface. It set off a dense cloud of debris that obscured everyone's vision for some moments before dissipating slowly.

"BETA here, one thing I'm noticing is a slight tingling. You getting this GAMMA?"

"GAMMA, same – it's kind of itchy."

"I'm not feeling it," reported DELTA.

"Get that ziplock ready, I'm scratching this now, but I can't seem to make…" Beta's voice was interrupted by an intense blast of sound. It warbled from low to high frequency with distinct groupings separated by very short intervals of silence.

"Agggghhhh!" Beta screamed in agony, dropping the screwdriver onto the ledge and pressing his gloved hands to his ears.

Jamieson shouted into the microphone over the background din. "Surface surface surface! Leave the scratchings!" He turned to address the others around the table. "We've got an emergency on our hands. Those divers will have no time for de-compression stops. Corporal Waring and Dive ALPHA, you'll be responsible for putting the three others into the hyperbaric tubes and de-vaccing to island base."

He turned to Lana and Matt. "As soon as those men have surfaced I'm shutting this mission down. We're dealing with forces we don't understand and have no resources to guide us. We're too small a team for this. Agreed?"

"Yes, leave as soon as possible," said Lana, realising that whatever she might say, Jamieson had already made up his mind and might have to be circumvented, "There's evidence of non-human technology, stuff we cannot explain. Now we may have stirred up a hornet's…" The sound emissions stopped as abruptly as they had started, leaving a palpable silence in their wake. "What do you think Matt?" she asked him again.

Matt had been fiddling with an audio recording device as the others were talking and was now playing it back on a separate monitor using an acoustic APP, showing the shape of the sound waveform. "It's definitely digital," he muttered to Lana. "Nothing like that could have been produced by a natural or biological source, but I don't think we need to…" He stopped when he saw her expression. She had tapped her forehead to warn him she had other intentions. "I mean," he said louder, "I think we need to get going, we can discuss this later."

The men around them were hastily picking up their personal stuff and heading towards the exit.

"Everyone get ready to board the choppers!" Jamieson checked the monitors. The three divers were already at the surface and in the process of taking off their gear with the help of their support team. "Hear this: all divers and support. You have no time before you de-vac. Leave all the equipment, everything and go. Those requiring re-compression must be in their tubes and be ready for the second chopper in less than five minutes. We'll need that second chopper back here as soon as the divers have been de-planed at base," he told someone else. "Go go go!"

Once they were outside the tent Lana turned to Matt. "Let's take a short walk. The chopper can't carry everyone at once, it'll be full enough without us – they won't notice. We can go in the second flight."

Once they were out of sight of the others, she took him by the arm. "Matt I know you've worked something out. I can tell from your expression. What is it?"

"Well, it's just a theory, but I am now convinced the sounds are counting down to some event."

"Counting down? How do you know that?"

Matt was forced to wait while the sound of a helicopter's blades warming up reached a crescendo and took off. "The recording I made of that sound emission lasted close to thirty seconds," he continued. "I can display it as a waveform on my laptop and when you enlarge the time base up to a couple of seconds you can see a series of rectangular boxes and notches in groups separated by a double width notch, which I think marks the time interval. If, as it appears, the boxes represent a numeral 'one' and the notches 'zero', when I checked the first number in the series it was the binary equivalent of 2450121. The numbers after it progressively reduced at an even rate until we got to the point when the sound stopped and the number at that point was 2428654. As I said, this reduction in time units occurred over a thirty second period that I measured. At that rate, I've calculated that the number will reach zero in about fifty-six minutes from the time the last emission was made. That leaves us with barely enough time to get out of here safely according to my calculations. So let's make this a short walk and be ready for that second helicopter?"

"Wow, so there's an intelligence in all this surely?"

"It can't be accidental."

"What do you think this countdown is for then?"

"I've no idea. We have no data whatsoever to indicate what the purpose is. We're in the realms of complete guesswork, but here's my suggestion. There's a ledge or threshold in the depths of this lake. It surrounds what appears to be a bottomless black hole, one that our sensors have been unable to plumb. What if this is some kind of extraterrestrial station or terminus? Suppose the sounds are a warning to stay clear of the place while whatever it is, is about to be transmitted or conveyed here, possibly through a worm-hole in space time? What might come through is anyone's guess. ET Invasion, global systems shut down. Who knows? Sounds like science fiction doesn't it?" Matt said, looking sheepish.

"I suppose that's right," Lana agreed. "I can't imagine Lieutenant Jamieson would buy such an idea. But you know what, this has made me change my mind about leaving. I'm going to stay and watch what happens."

"You can't be serious. Your life will be at risk!"

"I know we're leaving video cameras here, but I'm not at all confident in their rush to leave, the technicians have got the bases covered – the ones we really need to make a proper record. But I am quite determined to remain as eyewitness. I think something amazing is taking place here. Matt, you've got to support me on this and stay in contact with our mobiles. At least you'll have a proper live observer to see what happens."

"You're crazy. We've no idea what we're dealing with here but, if anything, I'd be interpreting that countdown as a warning to stay out of the way. You shouldn't risk your life to prove that one way or the other." He paused, seemingly torn with indecision himself. "Please don't do this! Stop playing the hero!" His voice cracked.

"For most of my adult life I've been waiting for an opportunity like this, Matt," she said soothingly. "It's why I joined D-SETI. I can't leave without doing the best I can to discover something that could be truly momentous. In any case, there needs to be someone to ensure whatever happens is recorded properly. I'm sorry Matt. My mind's made up. Now you're wasting time and could be risking others lives with your unnecessary delay. Please go and get in line for the return flight. If you see Jamieson, you can tell him I decided to go back via the access track instead of waiting for the helicopter. I'll keep you posted with the handheld."

Matt sighed like he knew Lana's mind was made up and there was no changing it, then he turned and made his way over the slippery rocks and scree, back to where the remaining soldiers were sorting out what if anything to take with them.

In the distance, Lana could already hear the sound of a helicopter coming back.

"What do you mean she went off by herself down the track? Is she crazy?" Jamieson looked like he wanted to tear Matt limb from limb.

"I couldn't force her to come back with us. She insisted she needed to check if there was anything else, below the lake or in town, which might throw some light on what's been happening here," Matt said, thinking up any excuse he hoped Jamieson would buy.

Jamieson shrugged his shoulders in angry frustration. "Well it's too late now. I can't afford to risk my men to go chasing after her. And here's the last chopper."

The helicopter was making an immediate turn around, leaving its blades still rotating at high velocity. Jamieson, Matt and the others ducked under the whirling blades and scrambled aboard. Almost immediately, the engines accelerated still louder until the craft lifted into a shallow banking turn, leaving the lake behind.

Lana suddenly felt an acute sense of loneliness at the empty site she'd taken over. What she had decided to do was irrevocable, irrational and dangerous. After she was out of sight of the choppers, she walked quickly back to the tent to see if there was anything she could do in the short time left before the countdown concluded. Matt had left a counter on the monitoring table and, as she re-entered the tent, his estimated time count was down to a hundred and eighty seconds.

Three short minutes. Holy Crap!

She checked that all the video monitors were correctly sited on their tripods along the shoreline, set to record the scene, then walked closer to the lake to where she felt she had the best chance of contacting Matt on her handheld, while also watching what was to happen more clearly.

She pressed the send button on her handheld. "Lana to Matt, are you receiving, over?"

Matt's voice was faint, masked by the sound of the helicopter's decelerating rotor. "Yes got you. Everything set up to record, okay?"

"Yes," said Lana, "I'm standing by the lake waiting to see what happens."

"That's not advisable, Lana, please think of your safety and move further back."

"You know me," Lana laughed, "have I ever erred on the side of…" A blast of sound interrupted her reply, and she lost all contact with Matt.

The almost deafening sound had a very different quality from the last countdown sample the team had recorded. It washed over her and she felt herself relax, as if in a waking trance. She could see herself outside her body, though no longer with the power to control it.

The lake had become covered with a misty blanket and through it she observed some human-like figures, others not so human, emerging from the water, up the rock strewn shoreline, before disappearing into the jungle beyond.

The sound subsided. Then she heard a whispering voice that had an aching familiarity. "Lana, it's me, come here, child." She vividly remembered at the age of seven, the anguish of losing her mother, after prolonged illness. Hearing her mother's voice in such an improbable context made her tremble with fear and overwhelming sadness, all over again.

It's a clever analysis of my deepest feelings, whatever this alien power wants of me, she thought.

She struggled to remain rational before losing her balance completely. Now, whether clever projection or reality, she was facing a most powerful need to meet again the one person in her life she'd loved so much and depended on for security and comfort.

"Can that be you mummy? It's been so long. What are you doing here?"

"I'm waiting here for you, Lana. Leave your clothes behind and just come. We are going on a journey together, further than you could ever imagine, and there's much to talk about."

In her dream-like state, Lana unfastened her clothes and let them drop around her. Then she carefully walked towards the lake disappearing into the mist without a sound.

"Well, she was right on one count," Jamieson said to Matt. "It appears that when you lost contact with her on her handheld, none of the recorders had anything useful to show us. All we have are more of these sounds and mist, that's all." Jamieson paused, allowing his anger to subside. "She still hasn't reported in?" he asked more gently.

"N-no, sir. I'm sorry, I did what I could but she wouldn't come. It was t-too late to argue, I had to leave her," Matt stammered, close to tears

Jamieson took pity on him. "We'll go and look for her, son. We'll find her." He ordered their single helicopter to return to Quarry Lake.

It took too long.

The tent and all the recording equipment were standing as though nothing had happened. There was no wind. The lake surface was glassy and untroubled. Apart from Lana's clothes strewn over the rocks, and one or two small footprints leading into the lake, there was no sign of her.

Divers ALPHA and DELTA were in their helicopter, so Jamieson ordered them to check the lake, hoping against hope that something might be found.

At minus fifty metres DELTA reported, "we've reached the ledge, except there's no ledge now, nor drop-off, just a flat bottom. It's completely changed. I don't understand..."

"Nor do we," snapped Jamieson. "And no sign of Lana?"

"No, I've made a careful search of the entire bottom and there's nothing here but rocks, mud and a lot of crab-shells."

"Okay, back to the surface, DELTA. Take your time."

ATTN: EXEC. D-SETI EXEC. CTEE. ASIA PAC.

Summary Findings Quarry Lake Deployment. PRIORITY: LOW
[Refer: Attachment 1: Report D-SETI Team Project Officer Quarry Lake CLASSIFIFED; Attachment 2: Report to ADF Special Ops. Quarry Lake, Sergeant Thomas Powell CLASSIFIED]

RECOMMENDED:

1: The Quarry Lake deployment resulted in no definitive evidence of extraterrestrial activity.

2: Confidential advice from Sergeant Thomas Powell, highly critical of the front-end decision to deploy and the execution of Quarry Lake deployment by staff of D-SETI, be noted.

3: Team Project Officer Matthew Armstrong's resignation, on grounds of ill health, be accepted.

4: All files connected with the Quarry Lake Deployment remain sealed for the statutory minimum period of thirty (30) years on the grounds of public interest.

5: Should any media request substantiation of rumours arising from events at Quarry Lake, whether relating to D-SETI or otherwise, enquiries are to be forwarded to: <u>General Harold Dilmer, Head of Australian Defence Special Projects</u>.

Rodney Jensen [rodney-jensen.com.au/wpz/] We're living in interesting times and growing more interesting as the future becomes the present. My journey into speculative fiction began with 'Conversations with Meidog', published on Amazon, a novel about the first contact with an extraterrestrial intelligence network. Its sequel, 'Camp X' is currently under review by a local publisher. My latest novel 'End State' a speculative fiction whodunnit is in beta stage and will be published in 2018. Besides fiction writing, I've had a professional career in urban design and related media and have contributed stories to The Australian, Sydney Morning Herald, Australian Property Investor, other journals and publications.

For at least in forgetting we get to move on.

'*Mad Island* was poisoned by plants'

by Becky Dales

Residents of a remote island off the coast of Queensland suffered 'psychedelic hallucinations' after being poisoned by a chemical found in local plants, an investigation has revealed.

Karmidin Island has been declared an official 'Do Not Travel' zone after a rare hallucinogen, N,N-Dimethyltryptamine (DMT), apparently caused locals to hear strange noises, including talking crabs, aliens and daemons.

"After an extensive investigation, we found high levels of DMT in many plants that grow naturally on the island," said General Harold Dilmer, Head of Australian Defence Special Projects.

"We believe the chemical contaminated the lake of an abandoned quarry and was then spread to islanders during a recent rain storm, sparking widespread delusions and paranoia."

Dilmer added that while the effects of DMT are intense and come on rapidly, they also don't last long.

The island and its inhabitants are expected to make a full recovery, though Dilmer couldn't advise when. Some residents have chosen to remain on the island, while others have been evacuated to the mainland. As yet, none have been available for comment.

Acknowledgements

Zena Shapter

We imagined a small island with an abandoned quarry, which was making a noise. It was summer and we decided that today was going to be the day a group of specialists from the mainland would finally arrive to investigate. The challenge was to explore this moment from multiple perspectives, and thereby comment on it as a whole as well as individually. We did it!

Thank you so much to the fantastic members of the Northern Beaches Writers' Group who contributed to this anthology. It would not have been possible without your generous imaginations, patient problem-solving, creativity, and collaborative spirit.

Thanks especially to editors Suzi Green, Chris Lake, Mijmark and Kylie Pfeiffer; to proofreaders Malibu Bert, Jacqui Brown, Alexandra Cain, Harriet Cunningham, Rose Saltman, and Sue Steggall; and to the Northern Beaches Writers' Group for helping set the strict parameters we then used to conceive this work. Your passion and dedication never fail to inspire me.

Finally, thank you to my family. Your support and acceptance are the backbone to everything I do. You know how I love books!

Zena Shapter

Also by the
NORTHERN BEACHES WRITERS' GROUP